For My Michael –
with all my love x ~ CF

For Nicole Ivett –
a real treasure! ~ BC

SIMON AND SCHUSTER

First published in Great Britain in 2012 by Simon and Schuster UK Ltd
1st Floor, 222 Gray's Inn Road, London WC1X 8HB
A CBS COMPANY

A CIP catalogue record for this book is available from
the British Library upon request

ISBN: 978-0-85707-264-1 (HB)
ISBN: 978-0-85707-265-8 (PB)
ISBN: 978-0-85707-882-7 (eBook)

Printed in China
9 10

Pirates Love Underpants

Claire Freedman & Ben Cort

SIMON AND SCHUSTER

London New York Sydney Toronto New Delhi

These pirates SO love underpants,
They're on a special quest
To find the fabled Pants of Gold,
For the Captain's treasure chest.

"Anchors aweigh!" the Captain cries,
"Hoist up Black Bloomer's sail!
Unfurl the secret treasure map,
Pants pirates NEVER fail!"

Black Bloomer bobs upon the waves,
The Captain shouts, "Hooray!
Sharks in fancy UNDERPANTS,
We've found Big Knickers Bay!"

The pirates grab their cutlasses,
And row their boats to shore.
But, "Yikes, me hearties, what is this?
Someone's been 'ere before!"

The footprints lead through shifting dunes,
Across the Three Pants Ridge.
Snap! Snap! snarl hungry crocodiles,
Beneath the Long-John Bridge!

The pirates wade through gurgling swamps,
Through caves as black as night.
They trek through prickly undergrowth,
Then, GULP! Oh, what a sight!

"We're here too late!" the pirates gasp.
"ANOTHER pirate crew!
They've found the golden underpants.
What are we going to do?"

The Captain has a cunning plan.
It's clever! It's fantastic!
"Grab their fancy underpants and . . .
CUT through the elastic!"

Sshh! As the rival pirates sleep,
They SNIP round on tip-toe.
But help! The Captain's parrot SQUAWKS,
And wakes them up – Oh no!

"Grab those pants!" the Captain roars.
"They're after us – oooh-arrr!"
But with their pants around their feet,
They don't get very far!

"Yo-ho! Ho-ho!" the pirates dance,
"Fine treasure fills our hold,
But what's the booty we love best?
The glittering PANTS OF GOLD!"

So when you put your pants on, CHECK,
The elastic is in place.
Or like those silly pirates found –
You'll have a bright red face!

Maths in Colour

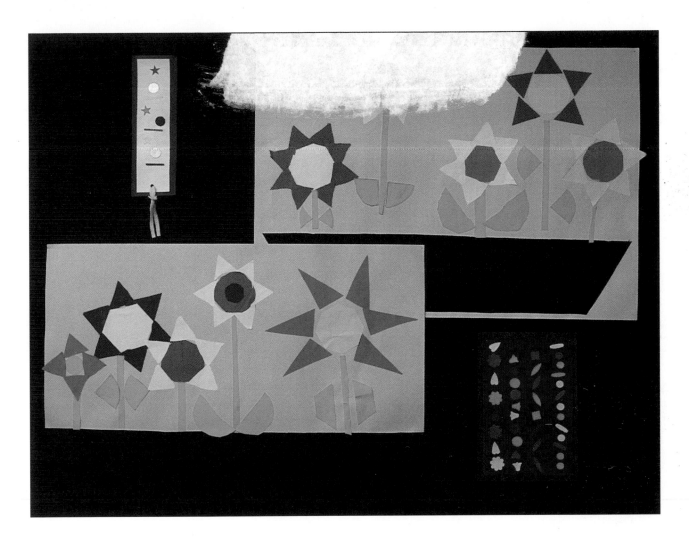

Wendy Clemson and David Clemson

Stanley Thornes (Publishers) Ltd

1

General introduction

Our intention in writing this book, is to give teachers starting points from which to develop children's mathematical thinking and knowledge through art and craft activities.

We would like to see mathematics and art enjoying equal status in the primary curriculum, and we know that there are many teachers who share our wish. In fact, in early years there seems little reason for avoiding giving art and other 'expressive arts' subjects, like drama and music, 'core' treatment; allowing the learning of mathematics, English and so on through them. The imperatives of the National Curriculum make it difficult for teachers in schools to envisage their treatment of what is to be learned along these lines. As a result, it may be that art and craft is squeezed in at the end of the day or week, or at the end of 'core' subject work. This disadvantages all children, for it gives them notions of how little society values cultural activities - art is unimportant. It also has a special effect on children who are not quick to perform the 'core' tasks asked of them, and those who choose to execute the challenges given to them at length. Thus, children who require forty-five minutes to do a 'twenty minute' mathematical investigation, and those who write a story taking four pages instead of a notional average of two, may simply not have the time to do any art and craft work that day or even during that week.

However, we think that we can help to reduce the likelihood that the 'expressive arts' become viewed by some as merely cathartic, therapeutic and even marginal, by pointing out some of the artistic possibilities in mathematics.

The mathematics in this book

All the activities in this book have associated or underlying mathematical ideas. They can be seen as part of an array of mathematical endeavours related to a topic or as a starting point for mathematical discussion. The activities have been placed under the headings which we felt most appropriate. Some activities could, however, have been included in a variety of locations throughout the book. For example, work on tessellation involves the study of a variety of plane shapes, and ordering things according to size also involves aspects of shape. The book is also split into broad sections which cover important mathematical concepts, such as 'Pattern and ordering', 'Angle' and 'Location and direction'.

Each of these has an introduction which explains the nature of the tasks covered.

While there is no intention of providing comprehensive coverage of all the mathematical concepts children should meet in the primary school, we are confident that we have included the important areas of mathematical thinking. We have also ensured that there are activities related to parts of the National Curriculum Programmes of Study for Key Stages 1 and 2.

The art in this book

We accept that there are a variety of ways of responding to our suggestions, where children may, for example, be asked to follow directions closely and carefully in order to demonstrate a mathematical point, or they may be asked to explore through art activity what can be done within a set of constraints. Either approach is acceptable. We are keen that teachers see this book as a source of inspiration rather than instruction.

We have tried to include activities which provide experience of elements of colour, pattern, texture and form (shape and structure). A variety of resources from both the manufactured and natural environments have been used in these activities. The book also provides opportunities for drawing, painting, print-making, modelling and design and construction.

We hope the photographs serve to demonstrate that the activities can produce a wide range of outcomes. Many of these are composite pictures which show the results of a number of related activities.

Resources

We have assumed that the children have access to the following resources:
Paper - sugar, plain white and of different weights
Card
Pencils, pencil crayons, wax crayons, felt-tip pens
Water colours, powder paint and brushes
Scissors, rulers
Glue for paper and fabrics
Containers for water.

Additional resources are listed on each page.

Contents

General introduction 2
Acknowledgements 4

Pattern and ordering

Introduction to pattern and ordering 5
Shape 6
Size 8
Number 10
Display 12

Measures

Introduction to measures 13
Length 14
Area 16
Capacity and volume 18
'Weight' 20
Time 22
Display 24

3-D shapes

Introduction to 3-D shapes 25
Cubes and cuboids 26
Spheres 28
Cylinders 30
Prisms and pyramids 32
Display 34

2-D shapes

Introduction to 2-D shapes 35
Squares 36
Rectangles 38
Circles 40
Triangles 42
Hexagons 44
Polygons 46
Tessellation 48
Display 50

Symmetry

Introduction to symmetry 51
Reflective symmetry 52
Rotational symmetry 54
Lines, axes and planes 56
Display 58

Angle

Introduction to angle 59
Right angles 60
Rotation 62
Curves and spirals 64
Mazes 66
Display 68

Location and direction

Introduction to location and direction 69
Left and right/up and down 70
Translation 72
Maps and co-ordinates 74
Trails 76
Display 78

Further reading 79

Acknowledgements

We should like to thank the following for their help with this book:

Davenham CE Primary School, Davenham, Cheshire (Julie Rowlinson and Jackie Stanway)

Hartford CP School, Hartford, Cheshire (Vikki Casson, Angela Graham-Smith, Gwen Robinson and Lynne Westworth.)

Overleigh St Mary's CE Primary School, Chester (all the teachers who lent us work from their displays, but especially: Jane Varah, Carol Vrlec, Chris Warburton)

Sandiway CP School, Sandiway, Cheshire (Helen Hillditch)

Leafield CE Primary School, Leafield, Oxfordshire (our long-time friend Helen Richards and her colleague Elizabeth Richardson)

Thank you too, to our daughter Frances, who helped to dissipate the tension when we were trying to take the photographs and whose comments and suggestions about our ideas and writing are always pertinent and insightful.

Introduction to pattern and ordering

Making patterns and exploring them seems to be an important part of being human. The noises and movements that babies make and repeat may be early pattern-making, rather than responses to information their senses are giving them about the world. If we ask children to look at, search for and listen to patterns, they may become more adept at identifying them and creating more complex patterns themselves.

Children need to be introduced to the notion that mathematics involves ideas about number and shape, and the patterns that can be made from these two elements. When children are pattern-making, if they are given opportunities to discuss evidence of pattern - how it continues, how it could be made complex and so on - this is sound support for the suggestion that their work is mathematical. It is important to note that pattern in a mathematical sense has elements that are or could be repeated; that is there is the possibility of prediction. Pattern searches and pattern-making should not occur only in art or mathematics sessions.

Shape
Patterns of shapes can be observed in the environment, for example, in fencing, tiling, borders, brickwork and paving. Such patterns may include tessellating shapes. The children could make patterns that replicate or use elements from the environment, as in leaf patterns. Alternatively, they could devise their own patterns. Methods of pattern-making in this section include potato prints and sticky-shape patterns.

Size
Placing in order of size is an idea that children are familiar with before they start school. In some of the activities in this section, they are required to use themselves and other people as sources for comparison. There are suggestions for comparing finger size and height. The concept of distance is introduced through drawing portraits, as well as the idea that picture size can be related to what it is we wish to show.

Provide the children with reproductions of miniatures, head and shoulders and full-length portraits. Also obtain a variety of posters to prompt discussion of letter size, impact and readability.

Comparisons of length and breadth could be made using paper strips, or brushes and brushstrokes of different sizes. The suggestions for geometric designs could lead to the discussion of length of line.

Number
The children themselves are the starting point for the first activity. 'Finger-prints' is used as a means of encouraging them to think about pattern in number - thumbs represent patterns of two, the digits on one hand the pattern of five and those on two hands the pattern of ten. 'Making books' is another craft activity with much underlying maths. The children's challenge could be to work out how many double sheets of paper are needed for the required number of pages and where the odd and even numbers occur. Patterns in the products of times tables can be shown using a hundred square and, for example, patterns of beads and circle patterns.

More complex number patterns are introduced through the use of Napier's rods. These allow the children to work out long multiplication sums. John Napier (1550-1617) was a Scottish mathematician, the inventor of logarithms and 'Napier's Bones', as he called them. Number-bond patterns are explored in the curved stitching activity.

Number systems other than our own provide children with new series of numerals to replicate, understand and use as the basis for invention. This is a potent way of helping them to understand the concept of a symbol. '2' does not mean anything, it denotes an idea or a number of objects. The Babylonian's sexagesimal system - where the idea of 60 minutes in an hour is thought to originate - is an example of an alternative number system.

First activities

1 Potato prints

Halve a potato. Cut a simple shape into one of the cut sides. Press this into a paint tray (made up as shown) and place it on a piece of paper. The children could combine prints to achieve different effects.

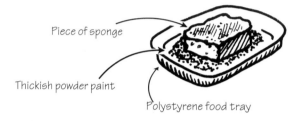

Piece of sponge

Thickish powder paint

Polystyrene food tray

Potato prints

2 Window-box sequences

Children could make flower-shaped card templates to cut around, and make the cut-outs into flowers. Create window-box displays, as below.

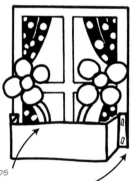

Card strips

Flower shape designed by a child

Card strip stapled and held off the wall

3 Sticky-shape patterns

Position sticky-paper shapes on to sugar paper to make repeat patterns. These appear as panels in the photograph below.

4 Pressed-leaf pictures

Collect leaves from the school garden or park. Before the leaves wilt, place them between sheets of newspaper and weight them down with a pile of books or heavy box. When they have been pressed for at least two weeks, remove them from the newspaper and arrange to make a shape picture. (See photograph opposite.)

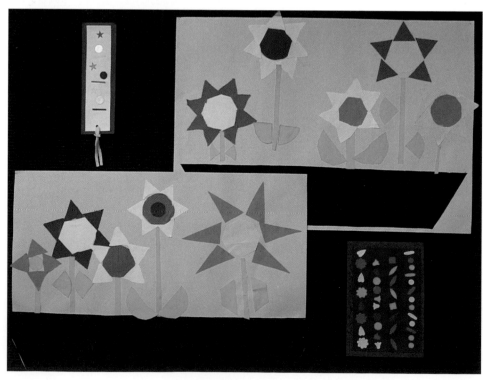

Further activities

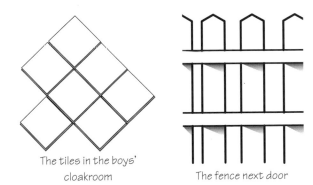

The tiles in the boys' cloakroom

The fence next door

1 Shape patterns around us

Look for patterns in the environment, for example, in leaf shapes, the arrangements of paving slabs, building constructions, fencing and flower petals. Encourage the children to try some observational drawing.

2 Building shape patterns

Start with a triangle, square or other base shape and build a pattern, see opposite.

3 Border patterns

Investigate the use of borders in a variety of cultures and in the past. For example, look at the borders created by the Ancient Greeks and the Victorians. Produce a single motif. Translate or rotate the motif as many times as necessary to make a border. The children could make frames for written work or pictures.

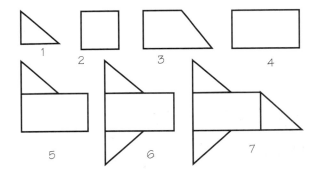

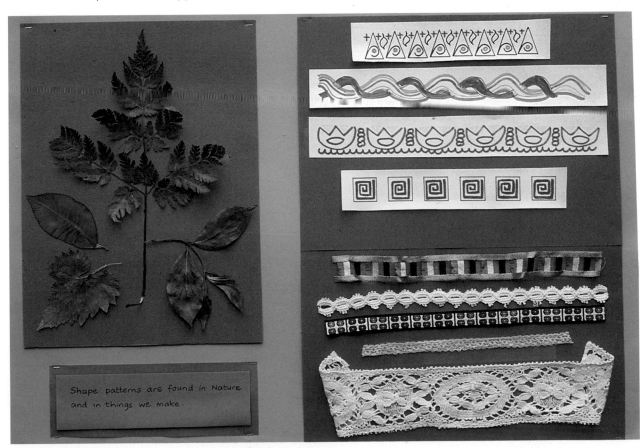

Shape patterns are found in Nature and in things we make.

7

Pattern and ordering - size

First activities

1 Fingers and finger puppets

Ask each child to draw around one of their hands and cut the fingers and thumb off their drawing. They could then place these in order, from largest to smallest, with a complete outline of a hand beside the digits, as shown below.

Baby   Thumb   Ring   Pointing   Middle

Finger puppets to match the length of each finger

2 Sizes of people

Organise a session where the children can draw around other children who are 5, 7, 9 and 11 years old and adults. Display the silhouettes.

3 Strip pictures

Make patterns using strips of sugar paper, tissue, cellophane, computer paper, brown paper, fabrics, ribbons and braids. Include strips of varying lengths and widths. (See photo opposite.)

Resources

Cellophane, fabric, ribbons, braids, paste, knitting needle, pasta shapes, different styles and sizes of lettering, cotton, picture frame, squared and isometric paper

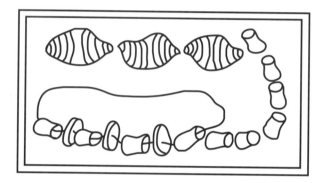

4 Jewellery

Make paper beads by winding long triangles of coloured paper around a pencil or knitting needle and gluing the ends of the paper with flour and water paste. Thread these on to cotton, interspersed with pasta shapes of varying sizes. The pasta can be painted and decorated.

5 Brush play

Try painting with brushes of varying widths.

8

3 Geometric line drawings
On squared or isometric paper, make geometric patterns using longer and longer straight lines.

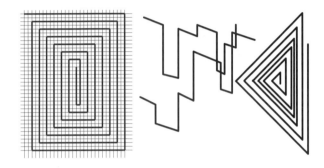

4 Getting bigger
Draw and cut out shapes of a variety of sizes. Superimpose them on one another.

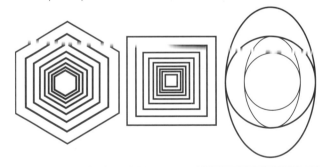

Further activities

1 Investigate lettering
Encourage the children to look at lettering on posters and signs. Design a poster for a school event.

2 In the frame
Make a card picture frame (or obtain an old picture frame). Ask the children to look through the frame and sketch a friend standing some distance away. The exercise can be repeated with the model standing closer, and finally closer still.

Concepts
Comparisons, measures, repeat patterns, regularity, estimation

Pattern and ordering - number

First activities

1 'Finger-prints'

Encourage the children to use poster paint placed on a sponge (in a tray or tub) or on their finger-tips to create prints. Make five colours of paint available. The children could make a print with each colour to produce a sequence of prints.

A worm - 6 fingerprints

2 Making books

Make some books. Decide on the number of pages. Demonstrate how to cut, assemble and number the pages. Identify odd and even page numbers.

3 Times tables

Identify patterns of products in times tables. Look for patterns in the last digits of the products. Present these on a circle or circular trail.

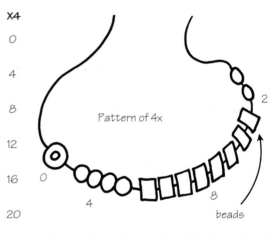

X4

0
4
8
12
16
20
24
28
32
36
40

Pattern of 4x

beads

Pattern of last digits is: 0, 4, 8, 2, 6, 0, 4, 8, 2, 6, 0

Circle pattern of 4x

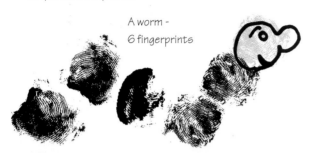

Number patterns in a hundred square

4 Hundred square

Colour in number patterns on a hundred square, e.g. counting in 2s, 3s, 4s etc. Display these as panels.

Further activities

Concepts

Sequencing, relationships between numbers, number patterns, number bonds

1 Number-bond stitching and times-table circles

Draw axes on card, marked at regular intervals. Join points on the axes with thread to make numbers, as shown.

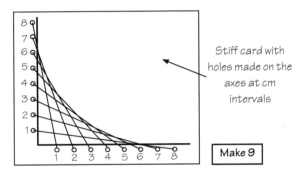

Stiff card with holes made on the axes at cm intervals

Make 9

2 Napier's rods

These can be made from card strips or lolly sticks. To use them for multiplication, set out the sticks that correspond to the number to be multiplied. Add the diagonals. The example shows how to find multiples of 79.

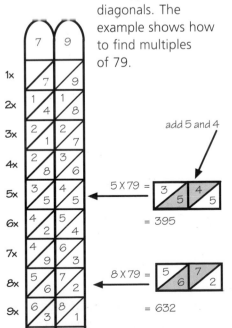

add 5 and 4

5 × 79 = | 3 | 4 |
          | 5| 5|

= 395

8 × 79 = | 5 | 7 |
          | 6| 2|

= 632

3 Different number systems

Find out how numerals are depicted in different cultures. Invent a system of notation and display its features in a 'number picture'.

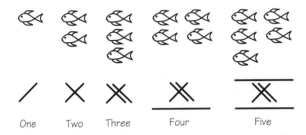

| One | Two | Three | Four | Five |

Once I caught a fish alive

Pattern and ordering - display

Some interactive display ideas

To give children a visual sense of order, include rows, columns, layers and compartments in displays. Make an interactive display inviting children to 'order' the objects. Create and add a puzzle book to the display.

Put all the first names in the class in order according to how many letters are in them.

Draw and name the playhouse toys in order of size.

Find a puzzle to do here.

Biggest
eyes

Smallest
eyes

Spiders to scare you.
Look in their eyes!

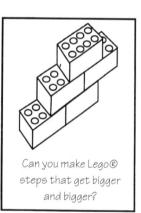

Can you make Lego®
steps that get bigger
and bigger?

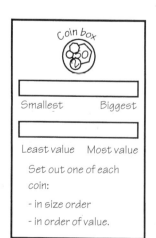

Coin box

Smallest   Biggest

Least value   Most value

Set out one of each coin:

- in size order

- in order of value.

Introduction to measures

Measurement is about comparison. The words we use in making comparisons, in carrying through standard measurement and in drawing conclusions about this information are of great importance. Discussion that takes place while the children work and after they have completed the various tasks will promote understanding of measurement.

The ability to make estimates is also of vital importance in gaining mathematical competence. Estimates are not guesses, for they rely on information the children already have about the kinds of comparison being made or units being used. They can estimate measurements when creating artwork, just as they do in other areas of life. How much paint to put in a pot, or what size of paper or fabric is needed are real-life decisions involving comparison, estimation and measurement.

Conservation of measurement can only be secured by giving children a wide variety of measuring challenges in a range of settings. In this section, we have set activities taking children from non-standard 'everyday' comparisons to work involving standard units and the use of appropriate instruments.

Length

Comparisons such as 'longer than' and 'shorter than' are important at this level. The dimensions of classroom objects could be compared to reinforce this vocabulary. The outside edges of objects and their silhouettes and shadows can be examined and discussed in relation to the concept of perimeter. Threads and yarns of a variety of lengths can be used in collage and in printing, and the idea of measuring length to achieve 'fit' underlies the work on bracelets, necklaces and other jewellery. Still-life drawing offers opportunities to discuss the varying heights of objects and how to make a pleasing composition. The concept of perspective can be introduced to the children when they make their first attempts at representing landscapes.

Area

Area is all about coverage. In relation to the children's own work, this concept could be approached as follows: 'How much paint is needed to cover...?', 'Is there paint under the top cover?' and 'Can we make prints which will cover a surface?'. These suggestions could be used to initiate discussion during the first activities.

Producing stencils provides opportunities for comparison of the area of a cut shape and the space it occupied. Space can be filled with cut shapes, as in 'Sticky pictures'. Making masks can be used as a means of introducing ideas about face area and coverage.

Capacity and volume

Capacity is often taken to mean, 'How much does it hold?'. In terms of, for example, filling a cup with liquid, we would talk about it being half-full, nearly empty and so on. Volume can also be taken to mean how much something holds, or how much space it takes up. The activities here address both aspects; the former in mixing paint, soft-toy making and making nesting figures; the latter in cooking and toy making.

Conservation of volume seems to be difficult to attain, for even as adults we sometimes have difficulty estimating the capacity of containers and volumes of liquids. However, a wide variety of experiences, both mathematical and artistic, can help the children to acquire ideas about capacity and volume that are important in everyday life.

'Weight'

This term has been written in inverted commas because what we measure when we weigh is actually mass. Making models with elastic media, like clay, will help the children to get to grips with the idea of conservation of 'weight'. When looking at the 'weights' of products available in supermarkets, the children are involved in work on packaging, advertising and product design. This area of study also offers opportunities for making paper collages, the discussion of abbreviations for measures and the kinds of quantities in which our foodstuffs are sold. Making balances and calibrating weights can also be seen as science or technology activities.

Time

Through these activities, the children are introduced to the concept of the passage of time and how we apportion it (day and night). They should also become familiar with the idea of past time, the present, future time (when birthdays will fall) and the use of devices to 'tell the time'.

Measures - length

First activities

1 Picture books

Make books, one 10cm long, another 50cm long and a third 1m long. Ask the children to find and draw things that are 'shorter than' or 'longer than' each book.

2 Outlines

Introduce the concept of perimeter by letting the children draw round things found in the classroom. Their classmates could try to identify objects from their outlines.

3 Yarn pictures

Provide a variety of wools, string, sewing thread and ribbon for making pictures.

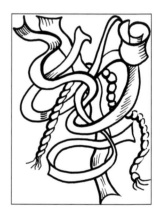

Which ribbon is the longest?

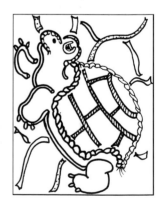

Can you see the tortoise?

Further activities

1 String blocks

Make blocks for printing using differing lengths of string.

2 Made to measure jewellery and headgear

Using the concept of perimeter, the children could measure their friends' wrists and make friendship bracelets from fabric or yarn. (See opposite.)

3 Relative height

The children could attempt still-life drawings to show relative height. Introduce them to landscape drawing and the problems of showing relative height at a distance.

Concepts

Comparison using appropriate vocabulary, estimation, standard and non-standard units, perimeter

Jersey fabric and fabric-covered card are ideal for making headbands and sweatbands.

Velcro fix ®

Necklaces can be made from leather thonging and pendants from clay or card.

3-way plait

Decorative stitching

Fabric glued on to card

Velcro fix ®

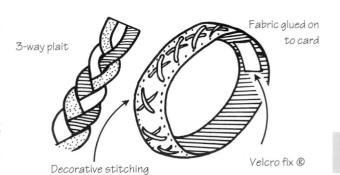

15

Measures - area

First activities

1 Surprise pictures

Rub different coloured crayons all over a piece of card. Paint over this thick layer of wax with Indian ink. When dry, scratch a picture on to the surface.

Resources

Indian ink, potatoes, junk material, leaves, squared paper, printing roller, fabric, paper sacks, sticky paper

2 Wrapping print

The children could print with junk material or potatoes to produce home-made wrapping paper.

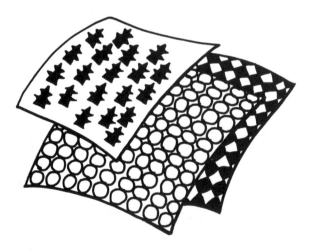

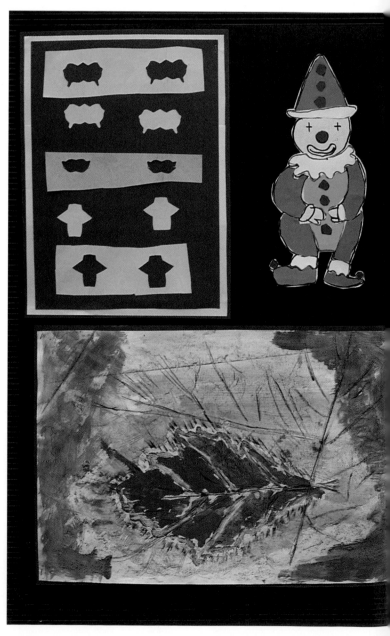

3 Leaf prints

Use a roller to apply a thin layer of paint to the underside of some leaves. Press each one on to paper to produce a print of its surface area. If squared paper is used for printing, the number of squares occupied by each leaf print can be counted - giving the surface area.

16

Further activities

1 Stencils

Cut out shapes from a piece of paper and paste them alongside the corresponding holes. Emphasise that the area of the cut-out and the corresponding shape cut into the paper are the same. (See photograph opposite.)

Holes   Cut-outs

2 Masks

Make masks to cover the face or whole head.

Face coverage

Thin card base, felt-tip pen decoration

Paint and fabric decoration on card base

Paper bag base

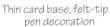

Paste down corners for snug fit

Whole head coverage

3 Sticky pictures

Draw an outline picture. Cut pieces of sticky paper to match regions of the picture. This could be achieved by tracing the outline of various parts of the picture on to different pieces of sticky paper. The finished picture will have its entire area covered. (See photograph opposite.)

Measures - capacity and volume

First activities

1 Pastry people

Make shortcrust pastry or buy it ready-made. The children could roll out the pastry and cut out shapes which resemble members of their families. Encourage them to inspect and compare uncooked and cooked shapes. (See photograph opposite.)

Uncooked pastry people

Cooked pastry people   *Their volume is bigger*

2 Paint trails

Fill a pot with paint up to a marked height. Use all the paint to make a trail or picture. Discuss the original volume of the paint in comparison to the paint on the paper.

10ml trail

10ml

10ml

10ml tree   10ml monster

18

Further activities

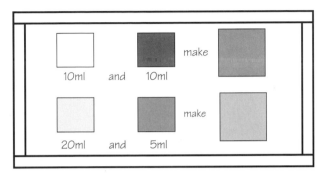

			make		
10ml	and	10ml			
20ml	and	5ml	make		

1 Paint mix

Allow children to mix exact quantities of powder paint to make colour charts, see above.

2 Soft toys

Make miniature soft toys. Draw around body-shaped templates on to felt. Cut out the shapes. Use different types of material (for example, lentils, soft wadding, rice, paper scraps, cut up tights) and varying amounts of these to fill the toys. Discuss capacity and volume in this context. (See the photograph opposite.)

Concepts

Comparison using appropriate vocabulary, internal space, space occupied, taking accurate measurements, diagonals

3 Nesting figures

Cut several circles of card, each of a different size. The children can make these into cones and decorate them. (They could also make nesting boxes, as in the photo opposite.)

staple

Gingerbread cutter

Cooked gingerbread

Can you make cone creatures?

Measures - 'weight'

First activities

1 Blob sculpture
Each child can create a model using the same mass of clay. (See photograph opposite.)

2 Which is heavier/lighter?
The children can make 'flap' books. They should begin by drawing something very light or very heavy and then create a series of pictures of objects in order of 'weight'.

3 Package collages
Paste paper labels on to giant models, in the form of a box, a paper bag and a can. Use these to discuss grammes and kilogrammes.

Resources

Clay, modelling boards, food packaging, weights, stapler, balsa wood, plastic bottles, junk materials, pebbles, encyclopedias, a balance

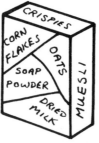

All these come in boxes

All these come in bags

All these come in cans

20

Further activities

1 Make a balance

Experiment with junk materials to make balances. (See photograph opposite.)

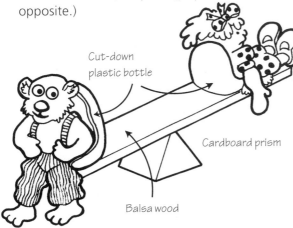

Cut-down plastic bottle

Cardboard prism

Balsa wood

2 Make weights

Paint pebbles. Calibrate them using a balance and weights. Label them accordingly.

Concepts

Comparison using appropriate vocabulary, mass, balance, standard units

3 Weighing records

The children could make a wallchart showing 'weight records' they have discovered.

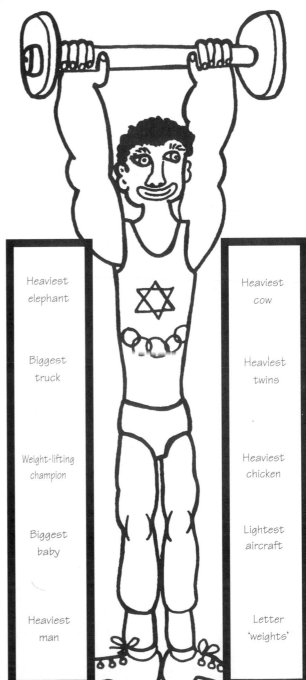

Heaviest elephant

Biggest truck

Weight-lifting champion

Biggest baby

Heaviest man

Heaviest cow

Heaviest twins

Heaviest chicken

Lightest aircraft

Letter 'weights'

21

Measures - time

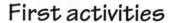

First activities

1 Day and night

Ask the children to draw pictures and think of words which relate to night and day happenings. Encourage them to make 'night pictures' black, grey or blue and 'day pictures' white, yellow or pastel colours. Use their work to create a display. Then, discuss the use of light and dark colours in paintings.

2 Day by day

Make concertina books so that the children can draw what they do each day, in sequence. Using pictures from educational catalogues, make a timetable for the activities which take place during the school week.

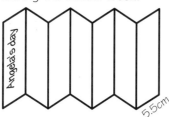

Angela's day

5.5cm

A3

Halve A3 sheet
(makes two books)

Here is what we do each day in school

| Monday | Tuesday | Wednesday | Thursday | Friday |

Today is

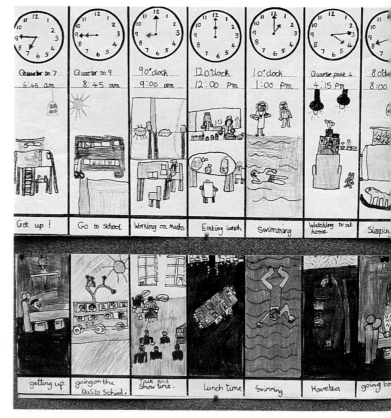

3 Seasons

Make a calendar based on the seasons. Use a combination of wax-resist pictures and collages made from found natural materials or fabrics. To make wax-resist pictures, draw a picture on to paper using a soft, white household candle and then paint over this with a water-colour wash. Charcoal or pastels are ideal for drawing silhouettes of the skyline in winter.

4 Months and birthdays

Make 'monthly calendars' for the children to colour in as time passes. Each child could paint and decorate a giant numeral to attach to the day and month of his/her birthday.

Marcus' birthday is on 11th January.

Are you older or younger than Marcus?

Further activities

1 Design a clock face

Look at a variety of clock faces. Discuss the need for regular intervals to be marked and how these are measured. Compare Arabic, Roman and digital numerals. Design and make clock faces.

2 Mark the passage of time

Chalk 'silhouettes' on the playground surface around shadow lines. Alternatively, suspend a cut-down plastic bottle filled with paint so that the paint drips out. Swing the bottle over large sheets of paper. Count the swings. How many swings make a second?

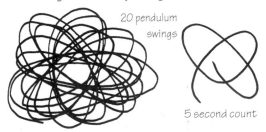

20 pendulum swings

5 second count

Measures - display

Convert a corridor, entrance hall or playhouse into a 'measures centre'. Display measuring instruments, photographs of adults at work using measures, children's work and home-made non-standard measures. Below are some ideas for interactive displays:

Here is a print made by the hind foot of a Tyrannosaurus Rex. Put your foot on top of it. How does it compare in length and width?

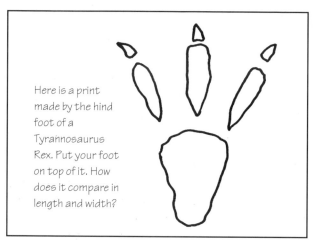

Here are three scarves. Tie the longest one around the longest snake. Which snake has the shortest scarf?

Which teacher wears the longest coat or jacket? Make a cardboard outline of the teacher wearing their coat.

Can you draw cartoons? Try drawing one in 20 seconds. Now, draw a whole strip of pictures in 10 minutes.

Introduction to 3-D shapes

Humans perceive the world as being three dimensional because they have binocular vision. Another characteristic of human beings is that they will attempt to organise and group what they perceive. Shape is viewed as a salient way of grouping. Some shapes have been found to have properties which make them ideal for use in rigid structures, others are used where economy of space is at a premium, yet others where flexibility is important. These ideas all have their starting points in the natural world.

In making their own intellectual maps of three-dimensional shapes, children need to handle them in a variety of guises and talk about them in their own words. They can describe these 'shapes', beginning with everyday words like 'sharp' and 'roly', alongside mathematical terms, such as cube, face and vertex.

It is important to note that there are only five <u>regular</u> three-dimensional shapes, and the most common of these is the cube. The others are the tetrahedron, octahedron, icosahedron and dodecahedron.

Cubes and cuboids

Cuboids are commonly seen in the built environment. Looking for evidence of cuboids in school buildings and in food packaging provides opportunities for discussion of the characteristics of these three-dimensional shapes.

There are many possibilities for using cuboids in art sessions, because they are invariably used for packaging. The children could pack a variety of shapes into a large carton to determine why cuboids are preferred. The activities in this section not only allow the children to work with these three-dimensional shapes but also to construct nets.

Spheres

A sphere is unusual because it has no plane faces. When a sphere is sliced through, the face across the cut is always a circle.

The first type of activity in this section involves model-making using spheres. The second type focuses on the representation of spheres in two-dimensional drawings.

Cylinders

As cylinders are used in packaging, these ready-made 'shapes' can be the base materials for model-making. The card tubes from paper kitchen towels, foil and toilet rolls are ideal for many of the craft activities suggested in this section. Though tree branches are not exact cylinders (they are in fact truncated cones), they do provide a useful natural material with which to work. This shape is also evident in some buildings. A study of the use of the column in architecture (which is also not always an exact cylinder) provides an activity to extend the best researchers in the primary school.

Prisms and pyramids

A prism is a solid shape with flat sides. It has the same shaped cross-section throughout its length. Prisms are common in the built environment, for example, roof shapes. Cubes are square-based prisms and cuboids can be either square- or rectangular-based prisms. However, we do tend to treat them separately from other kinds of prism.

A pyramid is a solid shape, with a plane shape bounded by straight lines as a base and its other faces meeting at a single vertex (the apex).

The activities in this section involve identifying and drawing prisms in the built environment and familiarising children with the attributes of prisms - by making models and nets. Pyramids are so uncommon in everyday life that the activities here have to be more contrived.

First activities

1 'Junk' models

Make models from packaging based on a theme. For example, build a model wildlife park or village street. Alternatively, base the model on a more abstract idea, such as 'things from the air'. Paint takes better if boxes are covered with blank newsprint first, or they can be opened out and made up again 'inside out'. If the boxes are remade, strong glue will be needed to stick the flaps down.

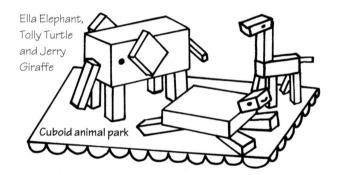

Ella Elephant, Tolly Turtle and Jerry Giraffe

Cuboid animal park

2 Carton puppets

Make these from milk or juice cartons. Before painting the waxed-paper cartons, dip them in washing-up liquid or stroke them with a potato. This will allow the paint to 'take'.

3 Peep-show

Use a shoe box to make a toy theatre. Cut out pictures from postcards and magazines. Paste them on the inside of the box to make a backdrop. Make cardboard figures and arrange these inside the box.

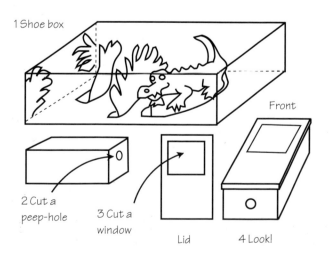

1 Shoe box

2 Cut a peep-hole

3 Cut a window

Lid

4 Look!

Front

4 Market stall

Make this from a shoe box, as shown below.

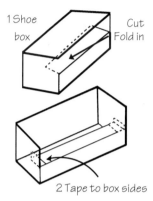

1 Shoe box

Cut
Fold in

2 Tape to box sides

4 Stick on box lid

3 Decorate

Resources

Packaging, milk or juice cartons, washing-up liquid, potato, shoe boxes, postcards, magazines, access to buildings, blank newsprint, squared paper, sticky shapes, sticky tape

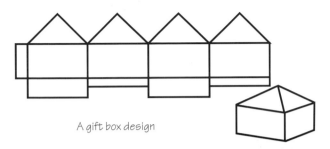

Further activities

A gift box design

Concepts

Face, vertex, rectangular prisms, nets, perspective

3 Drawing the built environment

Encourage the children to practise drawing any cuboid shapes that they can identify in the built environment.

1 Nets and boxes

Cut open some cartons and paste them down on to a piece of paper. Display the nets to show the shapes which they consist of. Using squared paper and card, the children could draw similar nets and then construct some cubes and cuboids.

2 Drawer

Ask the children to cut one end off a shoe box and use this as a drawer front. They can then make a drawer to fit inside the original shoe box and decorate the box with paper shapes or magazine pictures. (See photograph opposite.)

I made a cube out of cuxi. I pulled it out and I made a net and this is the shape. It has six squares in it.

3-D shapes - spheres

First activities

1 Clay paperweights

Each child rolls a ball of clay. The base of the ball should then be flattened so that it rests on a board. These paperweights could be decorated by making gentle impressions with sticks, straws, card and modelling tools - retaining the original shape of the ball of clay. The children should allow their paperweights to dry before painting and varnishing them.

2 Ping-Pong® puppets

Produce finger, card tube or stick puppets, as shown below.

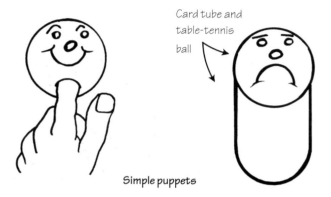

Card tube and table-tennis ball

Simple puppets

Felt hand

Glue piece of material back and front

Stick puppet

Pea stick

Further activities

1 Take a ball of paper

Screw up a large sheet of newspaper into a ball. Wrap this in another sheet of newspaper and then in a sheet of plain paper. Paste down the ends of the paper so that the ball shape is retained. Use this as the base shape for all kinds of creatures. (See photograph opposite.)

2 Bobbles

Create 'bobble creatures' using card circles and wool, as shown here. (See photograph opposite.)

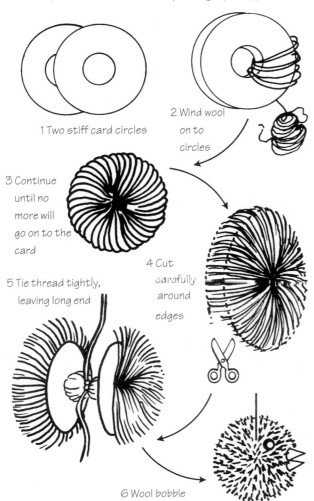

1 Two stiff card circles

2 Wind wool on to circles

3 Continue until no more will go on to the card

4 Cut carefully around edges

5 Tie thread tightly, leaving long end

6 Wool bobble

Makes good chicks, robins, hedgehogs

3 Drawing spheres

The children could attempt still-life drawings of fruit and vegetables, using pastels or charcoal. Shading of the objects should give a sense of 'solidity'.

4 Spherical models

Make a model of the Earth from a balloon and papier mâché, as shown here.

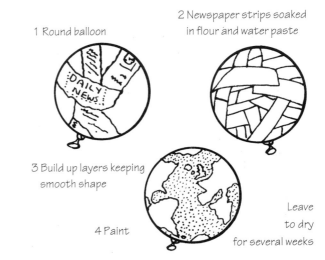

1 Round balloon

2 Newspaper strips soaked in flour and water paste

3 Build up layers keeping smooth shape

4 Paint

Leave to dry for several weeks

3-D shapes - cylinders

First activities

1 Totem pole

Decorate card tubes (from toilet or kitchen rolls) using coloured paper and fabric. Make vertical cuts in the tops and bottoms of the cylinders and slot them together.

2 A castle tower

Build a corrugated-card tower, big enough for a child to walk inside. Enact *Sleeping Beauty, Rapunzel* or the Norman invasion.

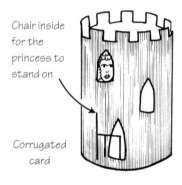

Chair inside for the princess to stand on

Corrugated card

Castle tower

Totem pole

3 Cylinder puppets

Make these from card tubes. The children could hold the puppets with their fingers or mount them on sticks.

4 Coil pots

Roll clay into sausages and twist these around a flat, circular base.

Base

Mould each coil to the one below

Resources

Cardboard tubes, glue, corrugated card, twigs, fabric, clay, tins, yarn, construction straws, grasses, bar of soap, books about doorways and columns

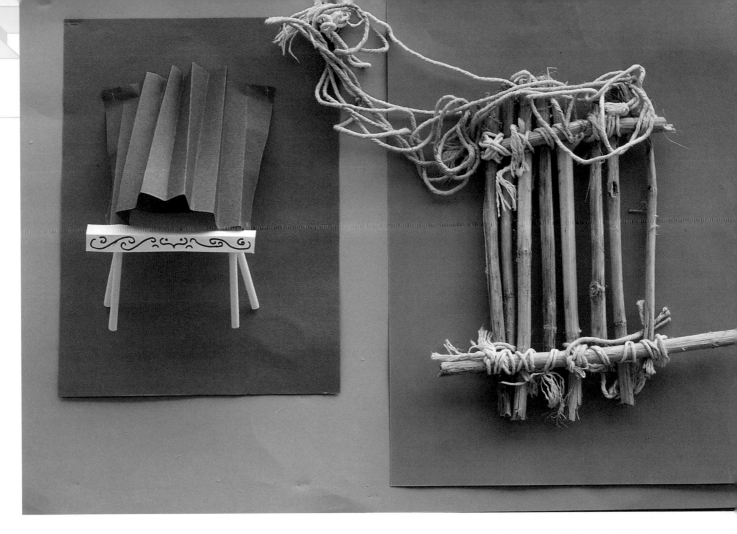

Further activities

1 Cover a tin

Demonstrate how to make a pencil pot. Obtain a cylindrical container without a sharp rim, like those that contain drinking chocolate. Wrap yarn or fabric around the tin and paste this down with strong glue. The tin will need to be measured carefully if a single piece of paper or fabric is used as a covering, see below. (Also, see photograph opposite.)

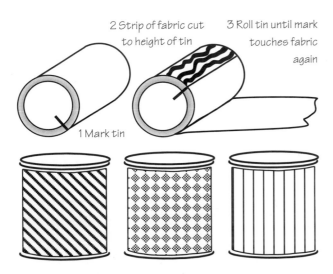

2 Strip of fabric cut to height of tin

3 Roll tin until mark touches fabric again

1 Mark tin

Concepts

Area, face, surface, spirals, volume and capacity

2 Take a twig

Create sculptures and collages from found twigs and grasses.

3 Construction straw art

Use construction straws to make models and in pictures.

4 Exits and entrances

Encourage the children to research doorways, porches and other entrances to buildings in the area. Focus on public buildings. Build porches and archways, using cylindrical paper tubes as verticals. Alternatively, research stone columns. Make a model of a column and decorate it appropriately. Try carving one out of a bar of soap. Note that classical Greek columns were not exact cylinders, as this shape looks distorted.

3-D shapes - prisms and pyramids

First activities

1 Find a prism

Children may find it difficult to recognise and name prisms, so collect a number to display. Table mats, gift boxes and chocolate boxes are sometimes triangular or hexagonal prisms. The children could then find and draw prisms in the built environment.

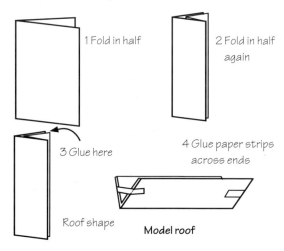

1 Fold in half

2 Fold in half again

3 Glue here

4 Glue paper strips across ends

Roof shape

Model roof

2 Triangular prisms

Show how these play an important role in some constructions by making model roofs, tents and feeding troughs.

Resources

Prism-shaped packaging, access to the built environment, construction straws, thread, clay/play dough

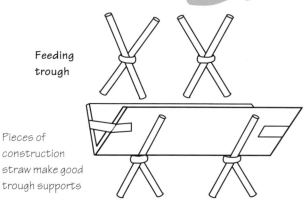

Feeding trough

Pieces of construction straw make good trough supports

Look at the school buildings. Where can you see prisms?

These sheep have faces like a tetrahedron! What shape is their trough?

Further activities

1 Pyramid mobile

Ask the children to draw a series of squares or equilateral triangles of different sizes. They should thread these on to a string in order of size, with the largest at the bottom. (The thread must go through the centre of each shape.) The corners of the shapes should then be joined with thread. Adult help may be needed to tie the thread from the corners of the bottom shape to the thread at the top of the stack.

2 Card pyramids

Design and make gift boxes, as shown here.

Concepts

Halves; kinds of triangles including equilateral, isosceles and scalene; squares, face, nets, structural strength, tetrahedrons

3 Soft pyramids

Each child could roll out a ball of clay or play dough and cut out a series of squares or equilateral triangles. These should be positioned one on top of the other in order of size, with the largest at the bottom, to make pyramids.

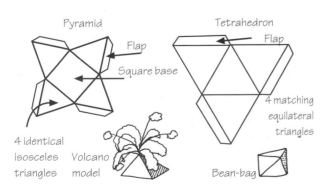

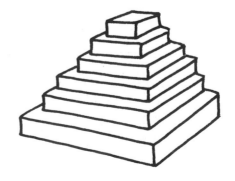

33

3-D shapes - display

Some interactive display ideas

Make a model of the school buildings and the surrounding environment. Discuss the shapes of the buildings, their relative sizes and aesthetic qualities.

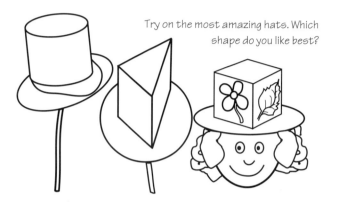

Try on the most amazing hats. Which shape do you like best?

Say which of these shapes would make the best:

plate, cup, drawing-board wheel.

Why?

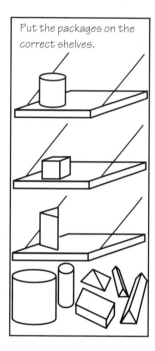

Put the packages on the correct shelves.

Make a 'net match' display using a felt board and 2-D shapes to press on it.

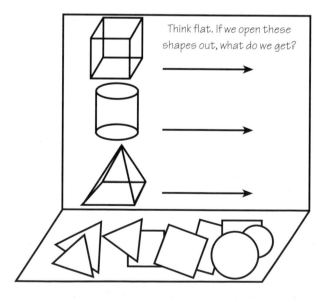

Think flat. If we open these shapes out, what do we get?

Cylinders and cuboids are good for model ma[...]

How many cylinders here?

34

Introduction to 2-D shapes

A mathematical understanding of two-dimensional shapes should not be merely the identification of, for example, triangles and squares. This work is important as it allows children to analyse patterns in terms of their constituents, however, the aim should be to enable them to become increasingly sophisticated in the ways they analyse and construct using shapes.

Squares

There are many ways in which squares can be used to form the basis of artwork. Materials such as fabrics and tiling - which incorporate square patterns - could be used for inspiration. The chequered boards on which traditional board games are played can also act as a starting point for activities. Alternatively, the children could be given a square of paper or 'squared' paper to work on. The outcomes should then be compared with those completed on rectangular pieces of paper - the shape of most pieces of paper and school books.

This section also provides an opportunity to investigate square numbers.

Rectangles

The activities we have chosen involve: drawing or folding paper to make rectangles, using a rectangular shape in picture- and card-making and looking at fractions of rectangles.

Circles

A circle is a set of points, in a plane, which are all equidistant from the centre. Pattern-making with circles, work with turning circles, craft-making using circles and semi-circles, the use of compasses and how to make a Spirograph® are all activities suggested in this section. Work in this area of study can be linked to 'rotation'.

Triangles

A triangle is any plane shape with three sides, so it is important that children meet a variety of triangles in the course of their work in order to identify specific types.

In this section, suggestions are given for the use of triangles in pattern-making and craft activities, and the presence of triangles in the built environment is investigated. There are also opportunities for completing work involving triangular parts of regular shapes, tessellating triangles and triangular numbers.

Hexagons

A hexagon is any plane shape with six straight sides. Regular hexagons, such as the shapes bees produce in honeycomb, have all sides the same length. (Although in truth, because they are three dimensional, what bees are actually creating are hexagonal prisms.)

Hexagons are also commonly used as the basis for patchwork, and the idea behind arranging them in this way is conveyed in 'Mats'. These can be compared with the tiles suggested under the theme 'Mazes'.

Polygons

This area of study provides an ideal starting point for work on two-dimensional shapes. The children can create any shapes they like - so long as they have straight sides - and arrange them in a pattern. 'Dotty' paper can be used, in the same way as a geo-board, to provide shape-making opportunities. We have included work on pentagrams and pentagons because these regular shapes have pattern-making potential.

Tessellation

This theme is a particular favourite of many teachers, and so although it could be categorized under other headings - for example, 'Triangles' or 'Hexagons' - we have set it down separately. The potential for eye-catching artwork is tremendous. Children will find it easier to work with squares or rectangles initially, before being introduced to more complex tessellating shapes. They could also experiment with semi-regular tessellations - where two shapes produce a tessellating pattern. Hexagons and triangles or squares and rectangles could be used for these pattern-making exercises.

2-D shapes - squares

First activities

1 Inventing with squares

Provide squares of paper, rather than rectangles, on which to paint and draw. The shape of the paper sometimes has a surprising effect on the outcomes. The children could follow this set of instructions. Fold a square of paper in half, and then in half again. Open the sheet out and draw a square in each quarter. Invent a picture for each section of the paper. (See opposite.)

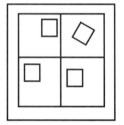

Make pictures using squares of sticky or sugar paper

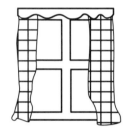

Patchwork curtains on a collage

2 Weaving squares

Collect fabrics with patterns based on squares - for example, ginghams and tartans - and show these to the children. Provide them with squared paper to colour in an alternating pattern, using two colours. The pattern could be replicated by weaving paper strips of the same two colours.

Resources

Sticky paper, fabrics with patterns based on squares, squared paper, corrugated card, balsa wood, Fimo®

3 Square prints

Make the base for a print block from a square of corrugated card or balsa wood. Stick pieces of card on to this to make a block. Dip the block in paint to make prints. (See photograph opposite.)

4 Square paper cuts

Using squares of sugar paper which are all the same size, show the children how to fold them in half (and into quarters if they wish). Ask them to cut a shape out of the folded paper and then open out the square. Display these as one large composite picture, or on a window.

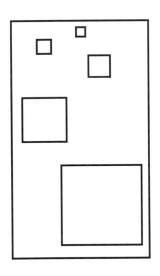
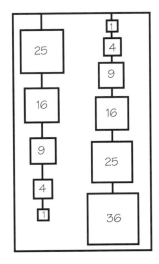

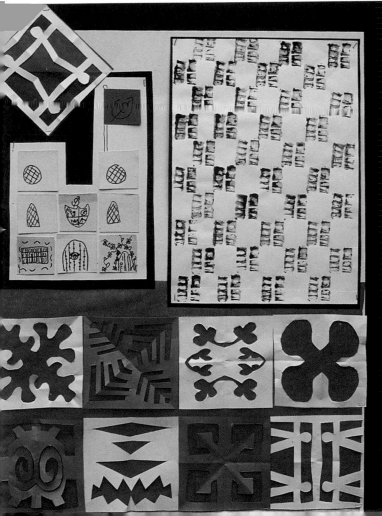

Concepts

Right angles, square numbers, polyominoes including:
3 squares (tromino), 4 squares (tetromino),
5 squares (pentomino)

Further activities

1 Square number mobile

Provide the children with 2cm squared paper. Ask them to colour a single square and then progressively bigger squares, counting the total number of coloured squares each time. This task demonstrates square numbers graphically. (See photograph opposite.)

2 Tiles

Make a cut-paper pattern, as in 'Square paper cuts'. Use this as a template and draw around it again and again. The cut shape can be rotated and reversed to give stunning effects. (See photograph opposite.)

3 Polyominoes

Provide the children with squared paper. Ask them to find as many configurations of 3, 4 or 5 squares as they can. These could be coloured, cut out and mounted on backing paper, or used in a collage. Note: In polyominoes, each square must touch the next along at least one side.

Polyominoes

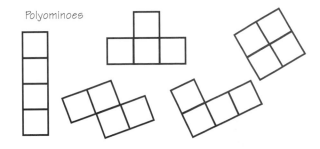

4 Make a game

Ask the children to devise a board game (either a strategy or track game) which uses a square board. They will need to work out how many squares are needed on the board and how big they will be. Playing pieces could be made from Fimo® or other modelling material.

2-D shapes - rectangles

First activities

1 Fan-folds
Ask the children to fold a piece of sugar paper - that has already been decorated - into a concertina. Point out how each fold makes another rectangle. Each concertina should be stapled at one end, opened out and displayed.

2 Fold and cut
Fold a strip of light-weight paper into a concertina. Cut out a shape, taking care not to cut across the width of the strip. Open out the strip and show it to the children.

3 Made from rectangles
Encourage the children to draw pictures which include only rectangles. (See photograph opposite.)

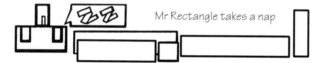

Mr Rectangle takes a nap

Bookshelf

High-rise flats

4 Greetings cards and postcards
Collect postcards and rectangular greetings cards. Make a 'picture wall', using the cards as 'bricks'. Create a variety of greetings cards for Mothers' Day, Easter and Christmas.

Window card

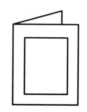

Cut-down shaped card

Ooh!

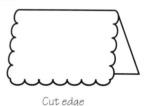

Cut edge

Further activities

1 Fractions

Create patterns from whole and cut-up rectangles.

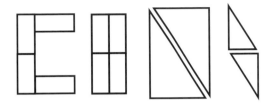

2 Paper hats

A simple paper hat can be made from a rectangle. (See photograph opposite.)

Basic paper hat

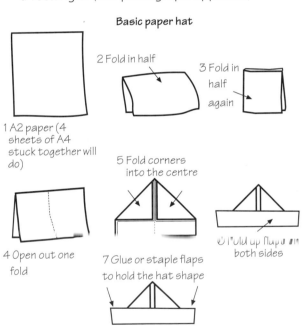

1 A2 paper (4 sheets of A4 stuck together will do)

2 Fold in half

3 Fold in half again

4 Open out one fold

5 Fold corners into the centre

6 Fold up flaps on both sides

7 Glue or staple flaps to hold the hat shape

Party hats

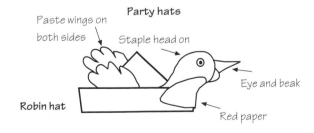

Paste wings on both sides

Staple head on

Eye and beak

Robin hat

Red paper

Christmas tree hat

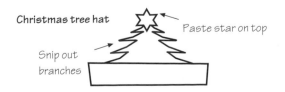

Paste star on top

Snip out branches

3 Golden rectangle

Draw portraits on different-sized pieces of paper, including one which has its dimensions based on the 'golden ratio' (8 : 13). Does this size look more pleasing? Research the sizes of famous portraits. How close are they to this ratio?

Resources

Stapler, postcards, greetings cards, books showing reproductions of famous portraits (with details of their sizes)

Concepts

Right angles, fractions, symmetry, matching, diagonals

2-D shapes - circles

First activities

1 Bubble prints

Make up some powder paint with equal amounts of water and washing-up liquid. Tip a little paint into a yoghurt pot. Blow carefully down a straw into the paint. When paint bubbles begin to well up, remove the straw and lay a sheet of paper on top of the pot. The outcome could be used as wrapping paper or to cover a book.

2 Top prints

Provide the children with bottle tops or circular lids for printing. Encourage them to make different-sized prints using a range of colours. (See photograph on opposite page.)

3 Turning circles

Make a 'choice' indicator. Cut out two circles of card, one larger than the other. Fix the circles together with a paper fastener. Below are different types of 'choice' indicators.

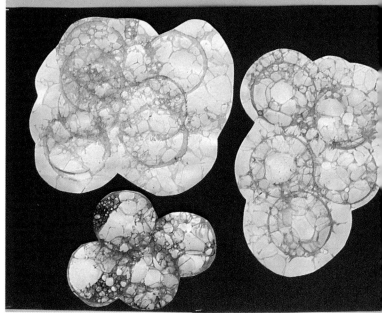

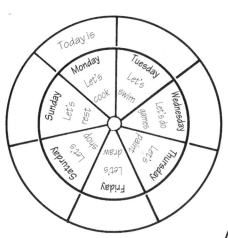

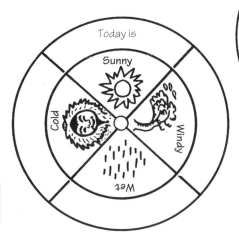

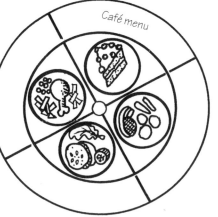

Resources

Washing-up liquid, yoghurt pots, straws, circular shapes, paper fastener, sponges, bottle tops, trays, corrugated card, compasses

Concepts

Rotation, fractions, curves, spirals

Further activities

1 Circle and semi-circle cards
The children could make novelty cards.

Christmas pudding

Get well

Horse shoe and four-leafed clover

2 Compass patterns
Provide each child with a pair of compasses to make patterns on a circle. (See photograph opposite.)

3 Spiral draw
Make a drawing aid from corrugated card. How close to an exact circle are the resultant drawings?

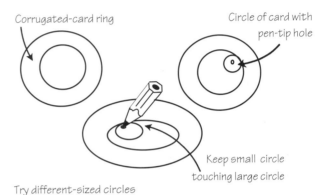

Corrugated-card ring

Circle of card with pen-tip hole

Keep small circle touching large circle

Try different-sized circles

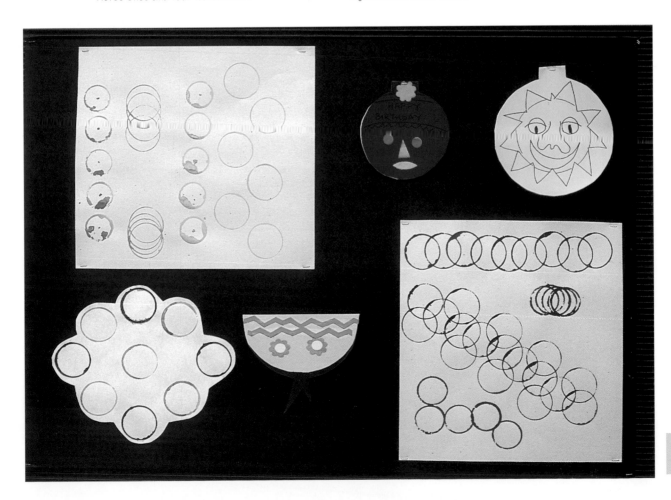

2-D shapes - triangles

First activities

1 Tumble-triangle patterns

Cut out a number of identical triangles and position them in a row. Rotate each one slightly before pasting it down.

2 Repeat triangles

Cut or tear triangles from paper. Lay them on to a piece of sugar paper. Paint over the entire sheet. Carefully remove the triangles. Allow the background paper to dry. Repeat the process using another set of triangles, laying them in different places. Use a second paint colour to cover the paper.

3 Find the triangles

Draw round templates of a variety of regular shapes. With a ruler, draw ways of dividing the shapes to produce triangles. Colour these.

Resources

2-D shape templates, construction straws, Plasticine®, clay, triangular 'dotty' paper, grid paper

4 Triangles in the built environment

Obtain pictures of roof supports and bridges. Encourage the children to identify triangles in these constructions. Draw and model them to find out why triangles are used.

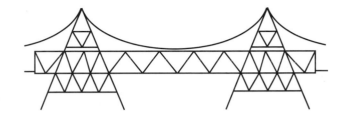

Further activities

1 Triangular numbers

Make triangular number constructions from Plasticine® or clay.

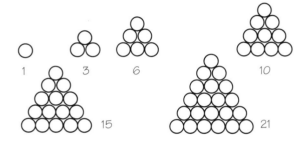

2 Triangle play

Provide the children with triangular 'dotty' paper and grid paper to create patterns and triangular trails. Ask them to colour these. Parallelograms, rhombi and larger and larger triangles will emerge in the patterns. (See opposite.)

3 Curl a triangle

Stroke paper triangles with the edge of a ruler and they will curl. The children can use these to make collages.

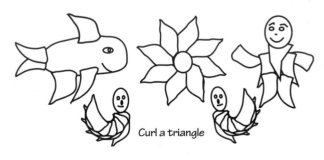

Curl a triangle

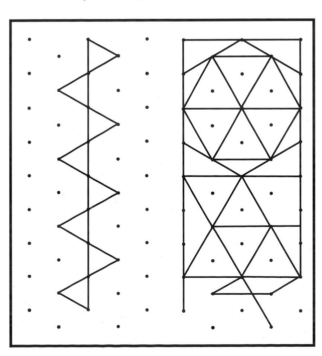

Concepts

Repeat patterns, angles, polygons, triangles, structural strength, triangular numbers

2-D shapes - hexagons

First activities

1 Bee on a honeycomb
Obtain some honeycomb for the children to inspect and draw. Then, make the display shown below from fabric, cellophane or sugar paper. Use a card template to ensure that the hexagons are regular. A bee can be made from tissue or felt, with net or tracing-paper wings.

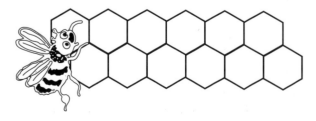

2 Spinners for playing games
Use hexagonal shapes to make spinners. These could have, for example, shapes, colours or numerals marked on them.

Concepts
Fractions, tessellation, hexagonal numbers

Further activities

1 Hexagonal numbers

Draw these using triangular 'dotty' paper.

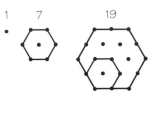  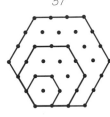

Draw and colour
to make patterns

Count the dots

2 'Mats'

Create hexagonal 'mats'. Cut out hexagons from card. Take one hexagon and draw on pathways which touch the centre of each side. The pathways should all be of the same width. Replicate this pattern on each 'mat'. Lay the mats down to make repeat patterns. (See photograph opposite.)

3 Fabric patchwork

Follow these directions to make a patchwork pattern.

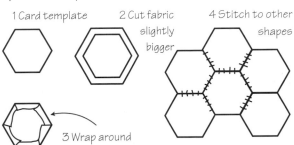

1 Card template   2 Cut fabric slightly bigger   4 Stitch to other shapes

3 Wrap around and glue or sew through

5 Remove card if stitched

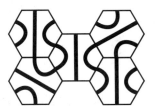

Design for 'mat'   Pattern continues from mat to mat

Resources

Hexagon templates, felt, spent matches, fabric scraps, cellophane, net, honeycomb, magnifiers, tissue paper, tracing paper, triangular 'dotty' paper, needles, thread

2-D shapes - polygons

First activities

1 Quadrilateral doodles

Provide the children with broad chalks or thick marker pens. Ask them to draw shapes with four straight sides, as shown in the photograph below.

2 Polygon paper

The children could practise cutting with scissors, making paper shapes with any number of straight sides. Ask them to paint on patterns that follow the edge of the shapes.

3 Join the dots

Offer the children square 'dotty' and triangular 'dotty' paper. Ask them to join the dots to make shapes. They could colour the shapes or regions within them. (See photograph opposite.)

Resources

Broad chalks, thick marker pens, square and triangular 'dotty' paper

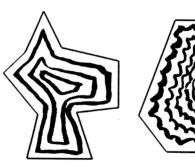

Concepts

Comparisons, quadrilaterals, regular and irregular shapes, pentagon

Further activities

1 Pentagons and pentagrams

Draw a variety of figures with five straight sides. How weird can a pentagon get? Ask the children to draw a really large pentagon with the diagonals marked. Challenge them to produce a pentagon within a pentagon.

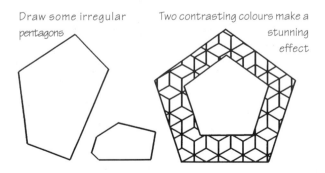

Draw some irregular pentagons

Two contrasting colours make a stunning effect

2 Septagon, Octagon, Nonagon, Decagon

Create patterns and constructions using shapes with increasing numbers of straight sides. Note that as the number of sides increases (for regular shapes), the resulting shape more closely resembles a circle.

3 Pentagonal numbers

Pentagonal numbers are made by adding square numbers to triangular numbers. Use triangular 'dotty' and square 'dotty' paper to represent these. Ask the children to count the dots in each pentagon.

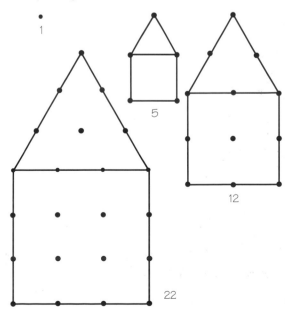

1

5

12

22

2-D shapes - tessellation

First activities

1 Pattern-making with shapes

Provide the children with ready-cut regular shapes including squares, rectangles, equilateral triangles and hexagons. They could make collage pictures from these, fitting the shapes together.

2 Shapes around us

Look for patterns in the environment. Draw or take photographs of these and make a quiz.

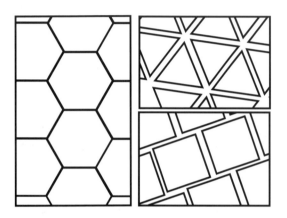

Where do you see these patterns?

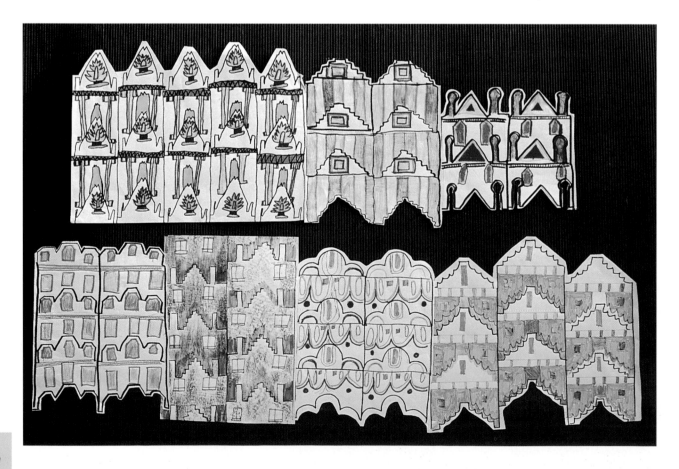

Further activities

1 Tessellating border

Cut out a square or rectangle of paper (6cm square or 3cm x 6cm). Cut a piece out of one side. Keep the piece and stick it on to the other side of the shape, as shown. Make a template of this shape from card. Draw around it again and again to create a border or frieze. Decorate the border.

Resources

Camera, film, ready-cut card shapes

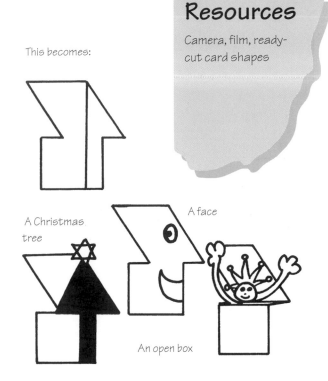

This becomes:

A Christmas tree

A face

An open box

Stick piece to other side

Remove piece

How to make frieze/border

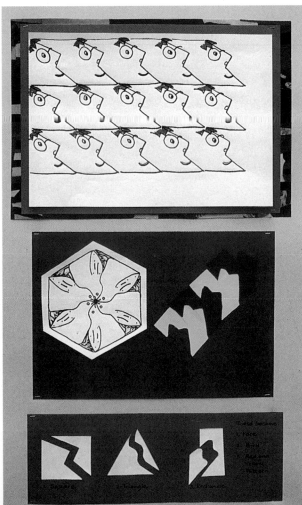

2 Complex tessellations

Complex tessellations can be made by moving the cut shape around a corner.

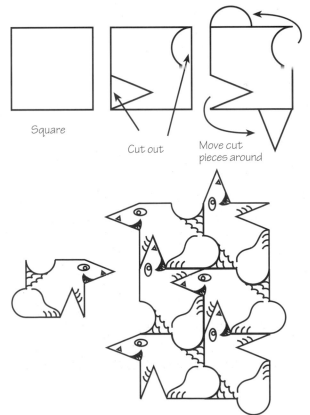

Square

Cut out

Move cut pieces around

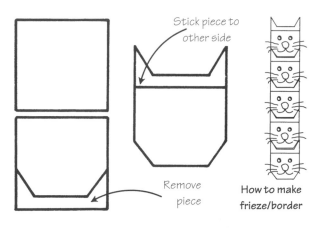

49

2-D shapes - display

Any flat surface in school can be used to display this work, for example, on tiles in the cloakroom, on the staffroom wall, on desk tops, floors and benches. Cover work with clear film if necessary.

School bench

Try letting a single display-shape lead a display.

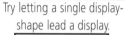

Look through the square window above. How many squares can you see?

Look at the circular pictures on display.

Make tessellating friezes to be displayed around several classrooms. Use the same starting shape for each, but try to vary the outcomes.

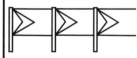

These are all based on a rectangle.

Introduction to symmetry

'Balance' or symmetry is very important because it affects the way in which we respond to the world around us. If a design or a structure is symmetrical, then it is often aesthetically pleasing. For this reason, humans make use of symmetry in fashion, art, architecture and design and technology. Symmetry is also widely found in the natural world - many living creatures have a broad (but not exact) symmetry. We can confirm this by covering half of our face and looking in the mirror.

During this work, children should be introduced to ideas about line or reflective symmetry and rotational symmetry.

Reflective symmetry

If a line can be drawn through a shape, giving two halves that are mirror images of one another, then it is said to have 'reflective symmetry'. Hence the fact that reflective symmetry is also sometimes called 'mirror' symmetry.

The children should be provided with opportunities, from the start of their school careers, to complete work involving reflective symmetry. Very appealing and eye-catching results can be produced from activities such as, cutting folded paper or making greeting cards. Viewing and replicating reflections in water increases children's awareness of reflective symmetry in the natural world. More complex pieces of artwork showing reflection can be composed using cut paper and logo designs.

Rotational symmetry

Rotational symmetry is shown when a shape can be turned part of a revolution and look the same as it did before turning. Examples of this are difficult to find and demonstrate to the children. Craft projects in this section aim to develop their awareness of 'match' which can be produced by turning. This work could be contrasted with that completed in 'Reflective symmetry' - involving matching halves in a picture or halves of an object. Note that many shapes that show rotational symmetry (including those we have used) also demonstrate reflective symmetry.

Lines, axes and planes

This is a consolidation and extension theme which draws on the work completed in both 'Reflective symmetry' and 'Rotational symmetry'. It is important for the children to recognise that 'lines' of symmetry are found in two-dimensional shapes - three-dimensional shapes have axes and planes of symmetry.

Symmetry - reflective symmetry

First activities

1 String trail

Fold a piece of paper in half and then open it out. Lay string that has been soaked in paint on one half. Fold the paper again and rub hard. Lay a drawing board on top of the paper. While one child holds the board steady, another can pull the string out. Open out the paper and leave it to dry.

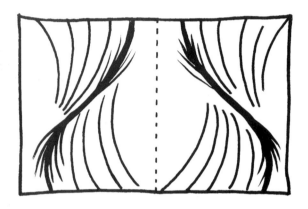

3 Mirror play

Draw a picture which has distinct halves. Allow the children to play with a mirror to create more pictures. They could then draw half a picture on plain or squared paper and use a mirror to complete it.

Resources

String, drawing board, 2-D shape templates, mirrors, squared paper

Mirror-play pictures

Use a mirror to complete the picture

2 Fold and cut

Cut out the following shapes from paper: squares, rectangles, hexagons, isosceles or equilateral triangles (or any other shapes that will fold exactly in half). Ask the children to fold these in half and then cut or tear patterns.

4 Greeting cards and decorations

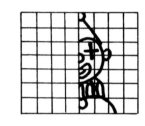

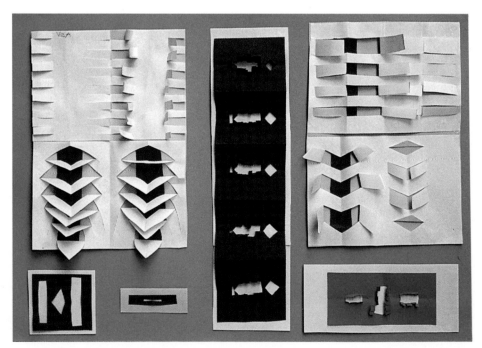

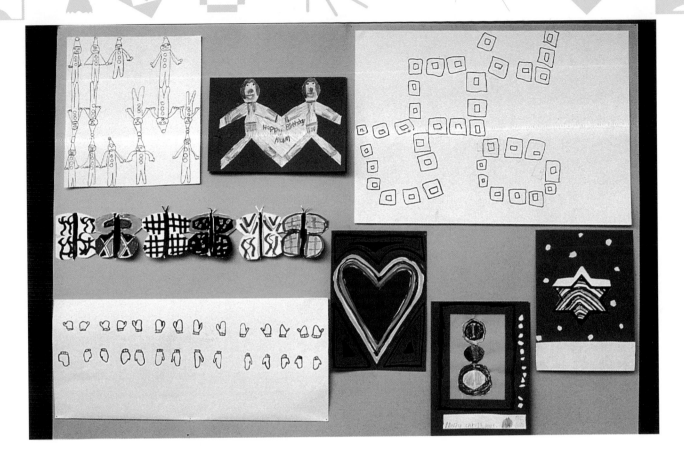

Further activities

1 Water pictures

Obtain some paper that is not too absorbent. Fold a sheet of it in half. Place it with the fold open crossways. Paint a lake, canal or river-bank on the top half. Wet the bottom half. Fold the paper over and stroke it gently. Open out the paper and show the children the 'reflection' that has been produced.

Concepts

Matching, mirror image, line/mirror symmetry, lines/axes and planes of symmetry

2 Logos

Invent a logo with matching halves for a school badge or a family or school event.

3 Patterns which 'match'

The children could try cutting a pattern into pieces and arranging it around a centre line.

A vase outline, decorated by pasting on and colouring shapes

53

First activities

1 Paper windmill
Make a windmill using light-weight paper.

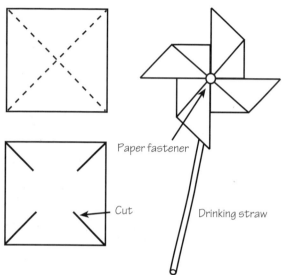

Paper fastener

Cut

Drinking straw

2 Snowflakes
Make snowflakes from tissue-paper, sugar-paper or sticky-paper circles.

Resources

Paper fastener, drinking straw, 2-D card shapes, sand tray, tissue paper, sticky paper, squared paper, binca, large needles, sewing thread, books about signs and symbols

4-way

Cut-out pattern

6-way

Cut-out pattern

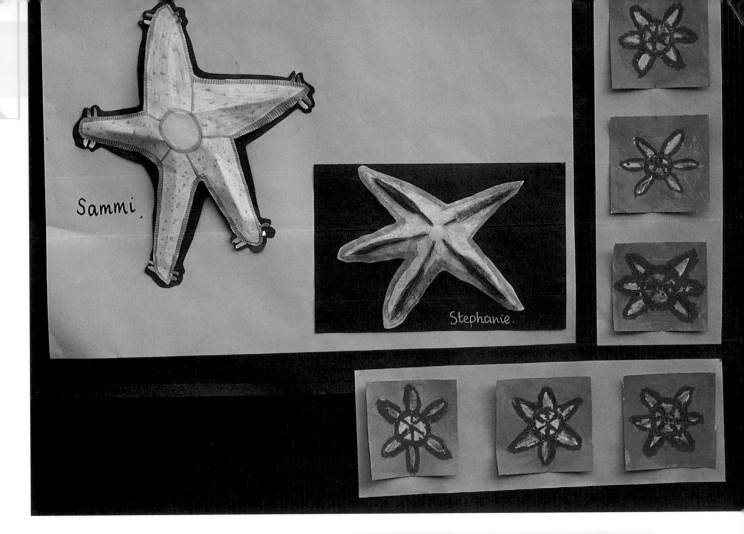

Further activities

1 Tiles

Make a simple cut across a square. Replicate this to form a tile pattern, as shown. Alternatively, cut a complex pattern from a square and display this.

Simple cut tile

Complex cut whole tile

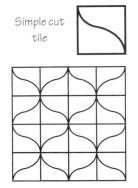

2 Cross-stitch

Design a pattern on squared paper. Transfer the pattern to fabric. (See photograph opposite.)

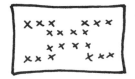

Concepts

Angle, turning, matching, lines/axes and planes of symmetry

3 Roundabouts and tops

Design a toy which looks the same from different directions. Model it using card. (See opposite.)

4 Symbols

Choose a symbolic shape, for example, the cross and explore its use in a variety of cultures.

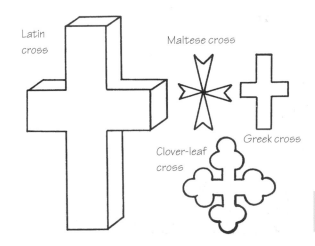

Latin cross

Maltese cross

Greek cross

Clover-leaf cross

Symmetry - lines, axes and planes

First activities

1 Matching halves

Take photographs of two or three children. Mount them alongside the faces of celebrities cut from magazines. Supply plane mirrors for the children to make faces with matching halves.

Take a mirror. Make a face

2 Plane shapes

Encourage the children to explore plane shapes using a mirror. Identify the lines of symmetry, and draw and label them on each shape.

Resources

Camera, film, magazines, plane mirrors, letters, numerals; books of flags, emblems and heraldic devices; clay, construction kits, straws

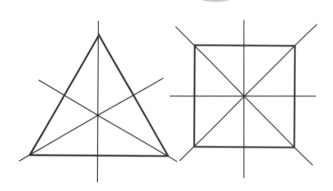

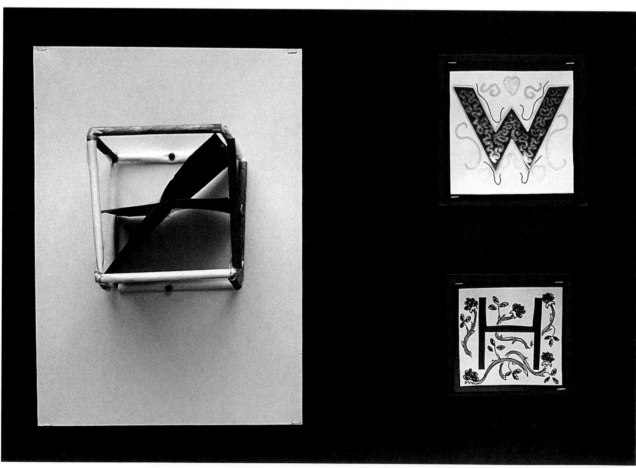

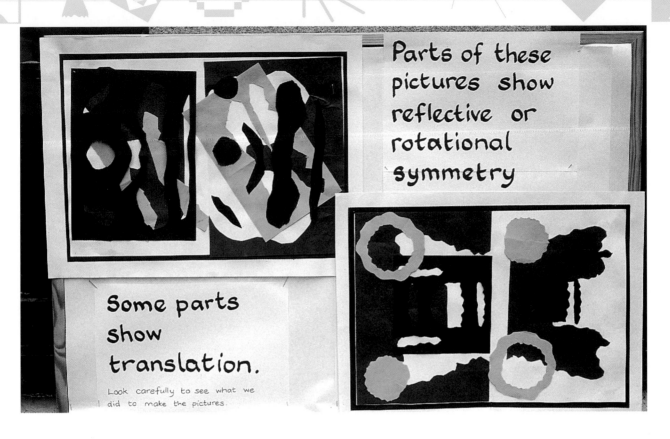

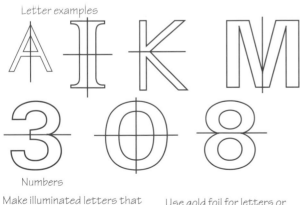

Some parts show translation.

Look carefully to see what we did to make the pictures.

Parts of these pictures show reflective or rotational symmetry

Further activities

1 Letters and numerals

Challenge the children to find the axes and lines of symmetry of various letters and numerals, as shown below and in the photograph opposite.

Letter examples

A I K M N

3 0 8

Numbers

Make illuminated letters that show symmetry

Use gold foil for letters or embellishments

2 3-D shapes

Make regular 3-D shapes from construction straws, drinking straws, construction kits or clay. Identify their planes of symmetry.

3 Flags and logos

Collect, inspect, draw and invent flags and logos. Identify and label their lines and axes of symmetry.

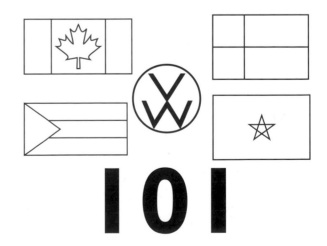

Concepts

2-D shapes, 3-D shapes, reflective symmetry, rotational symmetry

57

Symmetry - display

Use contrasting colours - for example, black and white or a 'cold' colour like blue and hot pink - to create a series of 'reflective' pictures. The colour contrast serves to emphasise what happens to the reflected shape.

Link this work to science by displaying a variety of reflective surfaces.

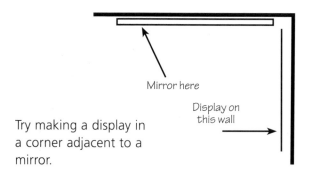

Mirror here

Display on this wall

Try making a display in a corner adjacent to a mirror.

In which of these can you see your face?

Draw what you can see.

Make a display of artefacts from another culture or civilisation. Identify patterns which have symmetry.

North American Indian patterns

Reflective Symmetry

Introduction to angle

It is important for the children to understand that angles are the result of movement - rotation. Rather than visualising an angle as a measure between lines joined at one end, encourage them to see it as the result of movement around one of the lines. Seeing angles as being a measure of rotation helps to establish the idea of a complete turn (360°), a straight angle (180°) and a right angle (90°).

Right angles

Right angles are commonly seen in the built environment - 'square' corners are apparent everywhere. The activities in this section emphasise the 'moving' aspect of angle, and include opening 'doors' and 'windows', right angles in human movement and those produced when home-made puppets are manipulated. Those materials used to create artwork that have right-angled corners - namely paper, mounts and frames - are also explored.

Rotation

Link this work to that completed in 'Rotational symmetry'. The mathematical idea of a complete rotation (360°) is the basis for this work. Rotation is demonstrated using colour spinners, star weaving and photography.

Curves and spirals

Link this work with that completed in 'Rotation'. Spirals (repeat rotations) occur in many forms in the natural world, for example, the centres of sunflowers, fir-cones, some animal horns and snails' shells. Curves are common in pattern-making too, and we have chosen arabesque, curvi-linear and Celtic patterns to demonstrate this. The children could research other similar patterns.

Mazes

The concept of a maze is the basis for many computer games. In this section, the children are encouraged to plan routes and pathways, for example, the longest, shortest and most direct routes, and those involving right-angle turns, right or left turns. This work involves strategic planning, spatial concepts and abstract model-making.

Angle - right angles

First activities

1 Corner faces

The children can fold a piece of paper, open it out and draw a face on the outside of the crease. Tape the faces to blocks or boxes.

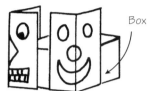

Block

Box

Sticky tape

2 Paper faces

Tear right-angle corners from pieces of paper. Paste these on to paper faces in appropriate places.

Mr Right-angle Nose

Miss Right-angle Eyes

Mrs Right-angle Smile

Baby Right-angle Ears

3 Open the door or window

Each child can fold a piece of paper in half to make a 'window' or 'door'. Draw a picture on the inside. Attach a 'hinge' to each door and window.

Resources

Blocks, boxes, socks, buttons, felt scraps, glue, craft knife, sticky tape

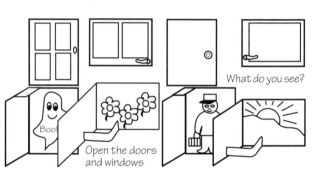

What do you see?

Boo!

Open the doors and windows

60

2 Frame it
Demonstrate how to measure up a picture for a frame. The children may need help when making their own frames.

3 Open-wide puppets
Make sock puppets. Use felt, buttons and wool for their features. Point out that when children hold a puppet's mouth wide open, there is a right angle between their thumb and fingers.

Further activities

1 Right-angle people
Mark right angles on a sheet of paper. Ask the children to draw people in active poses around them. They could then produce a strip-cartoon sequence involving a right-angle character.

Concepts

Rotation, part rotation, fractions, degrees

4 Box-corner collection or display
Invite the children to use a box corner to make a display or stand-up scene. The edges to the display corner can be cut square or in an irregular way, as shown below.

We looked everywhere

Rocks we found

Angle - rotation

First activities

1   Colour spinners

Circles of card can be coloured in different ways to produce colour-mix results when spun. Push a spent match through the centre of each circle to complete the spinners.

2   Rollo prints

Make a roller for printing, as shown below. Etch a pattern in the Plasticine®, and cover this surface in paint by rolling it in a paint tray. Transfer the print to paper. Afterwards, wash the Plasticine® very carefully or peel it off and mould on a fresh layer. Experiment with different coloured paints and overprinting.

Resources

Spent matches, cotton reel, Plasticine®, lolly sticks, wool, camera, film

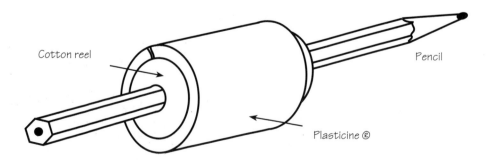

Cotton reel

Pencil

Plasticine ®

Further activities

1 Border print

Create a print suitable for the rim of a teacup or plate. (See photograph opposite.)

2 Star weaving

Glue two lolly sticks at right angles, as shown below. When the glue is dry, tie the end of a piece of wool around the centre of one of the sticks. Keeping the wool taut, wind it under and then right around the next stick. Do the same around the other two arms of the cross. Keep winding, making sure that there are no overlapping strands. Experiment with different coloured wools.

Concepts

Turning, repeat patterns, symmetry

3 Photographs all around

The children could take a series of photographs while standing on one spot. They should turn a little before taking each shot. Choose a location from which the photographs are to be taken, for example, from the centre of the playground or at the school gate. Display the results. Discuss what we 'see', what is 'there' and devices like the 'camera obscura'.

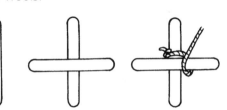
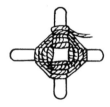
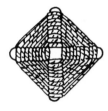

Angle - curves and spirals

First activities

1 Paper spirals

Cut spirals from circles or squares of fairly heavy-weight paper. Sugar paper or wallpaper is ideal for this.

These can be hung up for display

2 Spirals in nature

Make a collection of natural objects that show spirals, for example, snails' shells, fir-cones, sunflower heads and tendrils of plants such as sweet peas. Allow the children to handle these objects and draw them.

3 Curvy collage

Use a variety of threads and yarns to create collages. Washable PVA glue or Copydex® should be used to fix these materials.

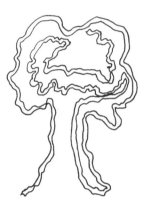

Resources

Templates, natural spiral objects, yarns, threads, fabric glue, squared paper, cork boards, curvi-linear arabesque and Celtic patterns, pins

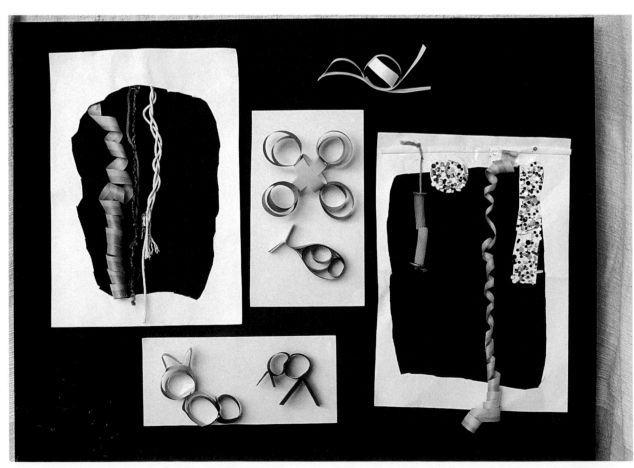

4 Making paper strips curve

Glue strips of paper in curvy shapes to make patterns and creatures.

Further activities

1 Arabesques

This is the name given to decoration which uses the rhythmic linear patterns of scrolling and interlacing foliage. Spirals and knots occur in these patterns, and they are probably Islamic in origin. Ask the children to invent similar patterns.

2 Curvi-linear art

This is found in some traditional art forms, from for example, Papua New Guinea. Encourage the children to create their own curvi-linear art.

Concepts

Repeat rotations, linking the concepts of 2-D and 3-D

3 Celtic knots

A Celtic knot is made from a single thread, and has been used for many centuries in a variety of cultures. The children could draw a Celtic knot on squared paper, using the pattern shown here as a model. Using a cork board, pins and macramé yarn or string, try to replicate this design. It is similar to a sailor's rope mat.

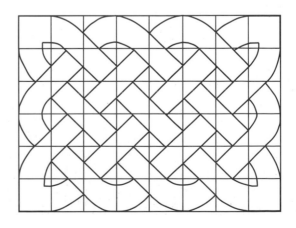

65

Angle - mazes

First activities

1 Plasticine® maze

Encourage the children to trail Plasticine®, clay or play dough 'sausages' to make maze shapes.

2 Toy maze

Using folded card strips of varying lengths, the children could create a maze for a small toy. The strips could be made to stand up by pressing them into Plasticine®.

3 Maze track games

Challenge the children to construct game boards based on a maze. These could be added to the school's resources.

4 Marble run

The children can design and construct marble runs, using boxes and card strips as base materials.

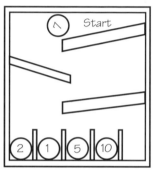

Marble score

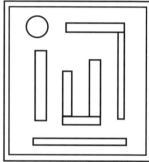

Marble maze

66

Further activities

1 Uni-cursal mazes

Draw and create a uni-cursal maze or labyrinth (which has only one route to the centre). Pebbles, clay and corrugated card could be used as base materials.

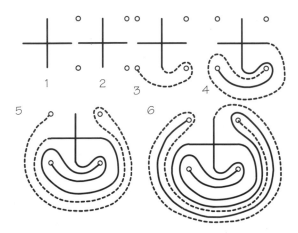

How to draw a uni-cursal maze

2 Multi-cursal mazes

The children could research this type of maze and draw some pictures based on real mazes.

Concepts

Turning, rotation, right angle, game rules, chance and probability

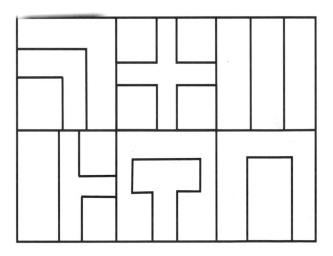

3 Maze tiles

Draw a series of maze tiles all the same size, which can be replicated. Make several copies of each tile pattern, and mount them on card. Lay them out to create novel mazes.

Angle - display

Ideas from this section are ideal for interactive displays, for angle is a movement. Invite children to turn a rotary pencil sharpener, wind-up a musical box, move the hands on a clock face and alter the leg or arm positions on a card figure.

Make Charlie do these actions. Look at the angles of his elbows and knees.

Display padlocks and screw-top jars, so that the children can work out the amount of turn that is needed to unlock the locks and open the jars. They can also identify the direction of turn.

The children will need to master a range of technical vocabulary in order to describe position and movement accurately. (The vocabulary covered in 'Rotation' and Angle can be linked to the work in this section.) As well as learning vocabulary, the children should begin to grasp the concepts of horizontal, vertical and perpendicular.

Left and right/up and down

Work on 'left' and 'right' could begin with discussion of hands and feet, and handedness and 'footedness'. Mirror pictures demonstrate the idea of reversal in images, and show reflective symmetry - that is the appearance of 'matching' left and right halves. Ideas that relate to the direction of working and of viewing the world are introduced through weaving activities and observational drawing.

Translation

Sliding shapes about is a common feature of some kinds of craftwork. Activities which give the children experience of translation, also provide them with examples of congruent shapes - which are the same shape and size. To produce multiples of shapes - which can then be shown to 'slide' about the page - the children are invited to do rubbings and cut out shapes. In screen printing, the shape positioned on the screen is 'moved through the screen' and appears on the print paper.

Maps and co-ordinates

Alongside the idea of a trail - which is a description of a route in words - the children should master the mathematical ideas behind map-making. The production of routes to school and pattern maps are introductory activities. Later activities cover the following ideas: plans, 'regions' of a map, co-ordinates and scale drawing.

Trails

Trails are included because they offer concrete experience of location and direction, and give the children opportunities to communicate action to others - in the form of directions - using keys and codes. The activities offer trails of the 'real' kind - for example, the photographic trail - and also imaginary ones, such as board games, where the children can choose to make games of chance or strategy.

Location and direction

First activities

1 Introducing left and right

Ask the children to draw and cut out giant footprints. They could have been made by a 'human' or monster, so long as they have a recognisable big toe. Fix them to the classroom floor to make it look as though a monster has walked through the room. Label each print 'left' or 'right'.

2 Handedness

The children can try writing and drawing with first one hand and then the other. They should compare the results.

Resources

Sticky tape, twigs, 'line patterned' fabric, construction straws, clay/play dough, magnifiers

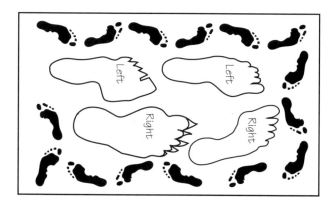

Do you use your right or left hand to write and draw?

Left   Left   Right   Right

Some people can draw well with their right <u>and</u> left hands.

3 'Mirror' pictures

Make paint 'butterflies' by folding paper, applying paint to one side, and then folding along the crease and rubbing hard (see below). Discuss left and right in this context.

Concepts

Pairs, orientation, symmetry, perspective, horizontal, vertical

2 Worm or bird's eye view

The children can imagine and draw, for example, the school garden from a ladybird's viewpoint or the playground as a bird sees it. Before the children begin, encourage them to use magnifiers to look down from first-floor windows, look up at buildings, inspect the ground and so on.

An insect looking at a grass tuft

Further activities

1 Up and down/side to side

Inspect fabric samples and patterns which show 'horizontal' and 'vertical' lines. Discuss this directional vocabulary. Create similar patterns by weaving or in collages. Make sculptures using materials which can be modelled to form a network, for example, construction straws, cardboard strips and found materials, such as grass stalks and twigs. (See photograph opposite and above.)

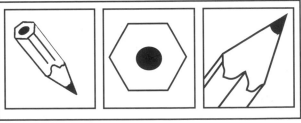

Pencil

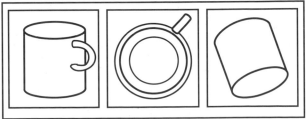

Mug

Draw everyday items from a variety of angles and display the results.

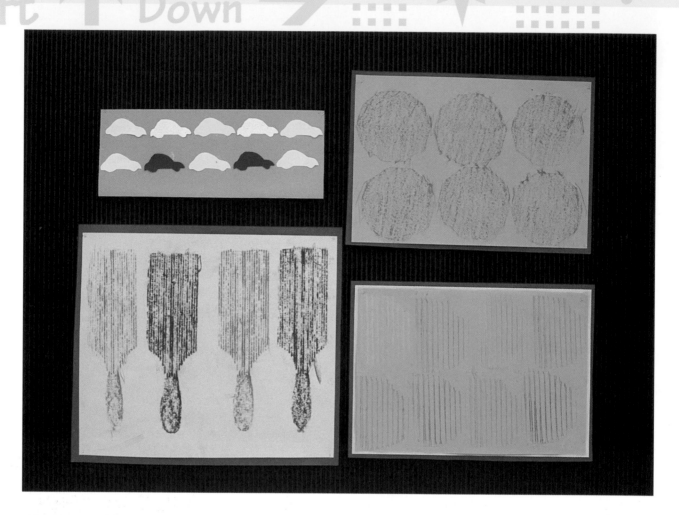

First activities

1 Rubbings

Find objects which have clear outlines and appealing textures for rubbing. Experiment with coins, ceramic tiles and cork mats. Make shapes from which to take rubbings by cutting up pieces of corrugated card, plastic netting and packaging. Rub each shape several times to give the impression that it is moving across the page.

2 Measuring strip

Make a measuring strip, counting strip or chart by drawing around and cutting out 'hands'.

3 Cut and stick

Fold a sheet of tissue paper again and again until there are many layers. Carefully cut out a shape. The shapes that are created should be pasted on to a sheet of paper so that they are all facing the same direction, as shown below. (See photograph above and opposite.)

Flags

Further activities

1 Screen printing

Make a stretched 'screen' from old curtain net and a picture frame. To stroke the paint through the mesh, use a flexible length of something like firm plastic or foam rubber (in commercially produced kits the 'squeegee' is a wide rubber strip held in a wooden holder). Follow the directions below. Note: mixed powder paint can be used, however, screen-printing inks are usually very smooth so as not to clog the mesh of the screen.

Concepts

Repeat patterns, shape and space, measures, including area

1 Stretch and pin fine, mesh fabric over a frame

2 Stick down masking tape on the upper side to protect the edges

4 Place paper shapes on the print paper

5 Dribble paint across mesh

3 Line up the printing paper below the frame

2 Using translation in composition

Dog show

6 Lay frame flat on paper and scrape paint across mesh

7 Paint will cover the paper, except where shapes are laid

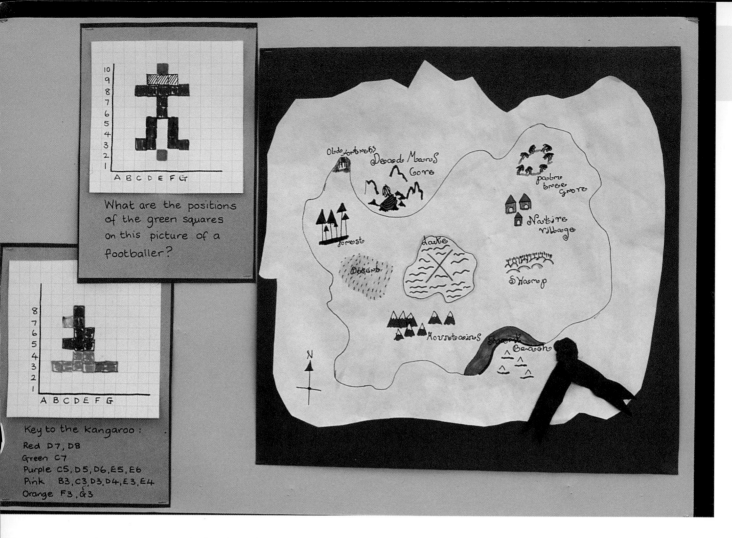

What are the positions of the green squares on this picture of a footballer?

Key to the kangaroo:

Red D7, D8
Green C7
Purple C5, D5, D6, E5, E6
Pink B3, C3, D3, D4, E3, E4
Orange F3, G3

First activities

1 Starting maps

Ask the children to draw a 'picture' of their route to school. Each child should describe the route shown in their picture and record this on tape. Display both pictures and the tape-recorder for an interactive display.

2 Introduction to elevation

Ask the children to draw the school buildings or other buildings from observation. Talk about our tendency to draw what we know to be there rather than what we see. Demonstrate how to represent the location and direction of parts of buildings when making 2-D drawings.

3 Pattern maps (introducing grids)

Provide the children with squared paper to create patterns, as shown below. Remind them to draw a key for their pattern map.

Resources

Tape-recorder, tapes, charcoal/pastels, coin, cartridge paper, cold tea, red ribbon and wax, books, maps, silver pen, thread, darning needle, squared paper

Make a pattern
A1 blue
A5 red
B2 ....

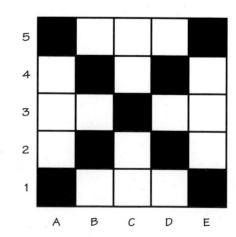

Further activities

1 Immerse cartridge paper in cold tea and leave to dry

2 Tear edges and draw map

3 Seal with red candle wax. Press coin or pencil into it. Glue on red ribbon

1 Treasure island

Make a treasure island map. (See opposite and above.)

2 Scale drawing using co-ordinates

Take a piece of squared paper and draw and label some axes, as shown. Draw a shape. Replicate this using squared paper with larger or smaller squares.

Concepts

Order and sequence, symmetry, mapping, elevation, scale, ratio

3 Star maps

The children can draw the stars in one of the constellations on card. They should make needle holes where the stars have been marked. These could be joined with silver thread or pen. Ask the children to draw a picture of the appropriate star sign around their star pattern. Mount these on a window and the star positions will show as points of light.

 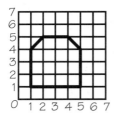

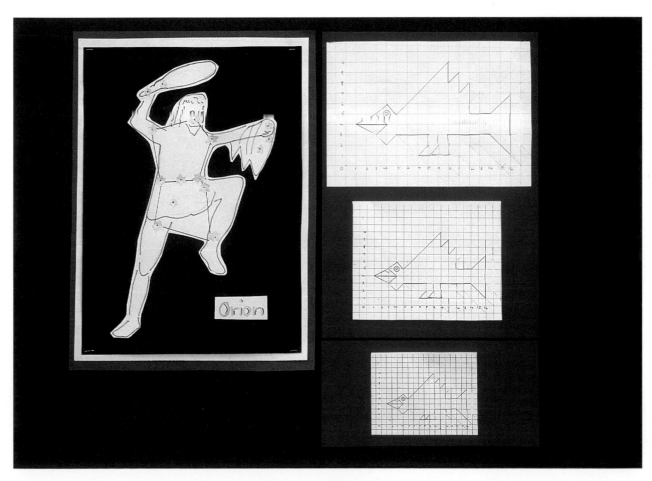

First activities

1 Rubbing trail
Allow the children to walk around the school and collect a series of rubbings, using sugar paper and wax crayons. Mount a display. Challenge other groups to 'decode' the trail.

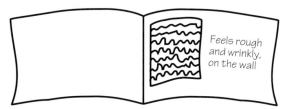

Feels rough and wrinkly, on the wall

2 Pacing trail
Encourage the children to pace out a trail and write an annotated guide to it.

School Trail

3 Imaginary trails
During story reading and writing sessions, encourage the children to invent stories about journeys they have made or would like to make. Travel books yield good examples to follow.

Resources
Stapler, travel books, story books, camera, film, a variety of board games

Trail key

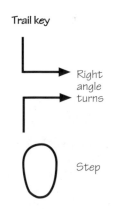

Right angle turns

Step

How many steps?

Take care

Stop! Look at the map again.

trails

Further activities

1 Photography trail

The children could take photographs around school and in the surrounding area. Suggest they use different camera angles to make the resulting pictures an intriguing puzzle for classmates, who could guess the locations.

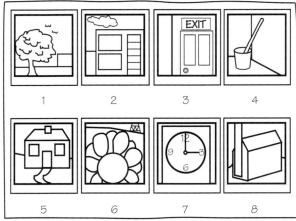

Ask if you can follow this trail

Concepts

Angle, rotation, mapping, signs and symbols, ordering, game design and rules

2 Board games

Collect a variety of board games to display, and let the children compare them to reach conclusions about common design features. Encourage them to design their own board games, which can be made up and played.

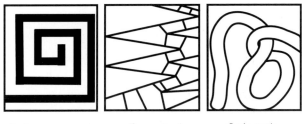

| Trail game around the board | Zigzag trail | Curly-path trail |

What happens to each shape to make the next one in the trail?

Location and direction - display

Displays can tempt children to alter their field and direction of view. Mount a display under a table, from the ceiling or down the side of a cupboard.

Invent a quiz which encourages the children to look around a variety of locations in school at a variety of heights. This kind of trail can be used for a treasure hunt.

Can you see what 'The Borrowers' might take from under the table?

Have you seen these on display.

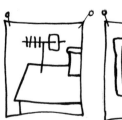

This picture is near to some water-pipes.

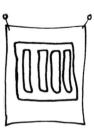

This is very high up.

Look for a figure in a doorway.

Look here!

Supply the children with magnifiers and binoculars with which to view the objects and pictures on display.

Further reading

Mathematics through Art and Design 6-13, A. Woodman and E. Albany, Unwin Hyman (1988).

Art 4 -11: Art in the Early Years of Schooling, editor: M. Morgan, Stanley Thornes Publishers (Simon and Schuster Education, 1991).

Start with Art: Developing Creativity in Young Children, S. Fitzsimmons, Stanley Thornes Publishers (Simon and Schuster Education, 1991).

Blueprints: Maths Key Stage 1: Teacher's Resource Book, W. Clemson and D. Clemson, Stanley Thornes Publishers (1992).

Blueprints: Maths Key Stage 2: Teacher's Resource Book, D. Clemson and W. Clemson, Stanley Thornes Publishers (1992).

Maths Investigations, D. Clemson and W. Clemson, Stanley Thornes Publishers (1995).

Also the Association of Teachers of Mathematics and the Mathematical Association produce a range of booklets and other resources.

First published in 1996 by:
Stanley Thornes (Publishers) Ltd
Ellenborough House
Wellington Street
CHELTENHAM GL50 1YW
England

98 99 00 / 10 9 8 7 6 5 4 3 2

A catalogue record for this book is available from the British Library.

ISBN 0-7487-1911-3

Printed and bound in China by Dah Hua Printing Press Co., Ltd.

Typeset by Aetos Ltd; Tadwick, Bath, Avon.